Th

MW01139993

<Murder in the Cotswolds>

James Ignizio

The Dog at the Gate

Cover Photo: *The Dog at the Gate*, Photographed by James Ignizio

October 2015

ISBN-13: 978-1517370664
ISBN-10: 1517370663

CONTENTS

Chapter 1

Aberdeen, Scotland; Thursday, 15 April 2010: The mouse, its curiosity piqued, circled the body lying on the kitchen floor. On its second pass the inquisitive rodent paused as it reached a position about six inches from the head.

Inside that head, the head of David Wallace – thirty-two years old and recently divorced, were flashes of semi-consciousness, punctuated by an intense, throbbing pain. David struggled to open one eye, then the other, and, having accomplished that feat, found himself face-to-face with the mouse. The tiny creature scurried backwards, performed a mid-air pirouette, and then raced to its hiding place behind a bureau in the bedroom of the sparsely furnished flat.

David fought to regain full consciousness and, once having achieved that goal, immediately regretted the effort. It was as if there was someone or something inside his skull beating a war drum. Glancing at his wristwatch, David saw that it was a little past six in the morning. The pounding in his head, coupled with what felt and tasted like a mouth full of cotton, was almost enough to make David regret his nine hours of binge drinking.

Struggling to his feet, David attempted a few wobbly steps and then, exhausted by the effort, sat down heavily on one of the two battered kitchen table chairs. There, arrayed in front of him on the table's badly chipped Formica surface, were the perpetrators of his discomfort: eight empty Old Speckled Hen beer cans and a half-empty bottle of whiskey – McIvor Scotch whiskey to be precise.

Until six months ago, David Wallace had only consumed liquor, in whatever its form, at social gatherings. Even then his drinking had been in moderation. For the past three months, however, he had discovered that alcohol – and lots of it – seemed to be the only way to relieve his pain ... and anger.

Pouring himself another glass of whiskey, David happened to glance at the calendar on the wall of the kitchen. It was Thursday, April 15th, meaning that it had been precisely three weeks since his divorce had become final and a little more than five months since he had been fired from his job. He blamed both of those life-altering events on his former boss, the man who was now sleeping with Monica, David's ex-wife.

The divorce and loss of employment had left David with a mounting stack of debts. He was now two months behind on his rent and his savings had dwindled to something less than four hundred pounds sterling. That came to roughly six hundred U.S. dollars in what he considered "real money" – and likely not even enough to purchase an economy class, one-way airline ticket back to Texas.

As David raised the glass of whiskey to his lips, his mobile phone rang. Who, he wondered, would be calling him? Could it be Monica? Might she just possibly want to reconcile? And what should he say if that were the case?

"Hello," said David.

It wasn't Monica. Instead, David's greeting was answered by a man's voice – a man who said his name was Dylan Jones.

David was having a hard time understanding the caller. The man, Dylan Jones, had a Welsh accent and seemed to be speaking abnormally fast. That, coupled with David's hangover, made it difficult to comprehend just what the man wanted. All that David could decipher at first was that someone – an "Aunt Rebecca" – had evidently died.

Who the hell, thought David, is "Aunt Rebecca?"

After several unsuccessful attempts to engage David in conversation – or at least a coherent conversation – the caller became more and more frustrated.

"Is this not David Wallace, formerly of Bent Spur, Texas – and now living in Aberdeen, Scotland?" asked the man.

"Yes," David replied, having finally gathered his wits. "This is he, and I'm truly sorry that this Rebecca person has passed on, but honestly, I don't recall ever having an Aunt Rebecca. And please, if you will, speak a bit slower. I'm having a difficult time understanding you."

Dylan Jones sighed, then – making a determined effort to speak as slow as he could manage – responded. "According to my conversations with Miss Rebecca, Miss Rebecca Fleming to be precise, she was your great aunt. She was in fact the sister of your maternal grandmother. She even showed me a photo of you and your mother, taken when she visited the both of you in Texas. Judging from the picture, I'd say you were about six or seven years old at the time."

Searching his memory, it suddenly came to him; there had indeed been a visit from a woman who his mother called, Aunt *Becky*. She must have been the Aunt Rebecca to whom the man on the phone was referring.

"Ah," said David, "I do remember her visit. I was six years old at the time."

What David didn't say was that he remembered Aunt Becky – or Rebecca if you will – had at first frightened him. Even though the woman wore long-sleeved blouses, they failed to cover the ugly scars on the back of her hands. And there had been something about her face that he, a boy of six, found unsettling. Nor did he mention the fact that, just a year following that visit, his mother had died and his world had been turned upside down.

"Good," said Dylan Jones. "Mr. Wallace, I'm the executor of your late aunt's estate. I'm calling to inform you that you are her *sole* heir. She has left *everything* to you, her home, its furnishings, her motorcar, and a modest amount in a savings account."

David was stunned. "Are you sure? Really, I barely remember the woman and only recall seeing her once, and that was about a quarter century ago."

"I'm quite sure, Mr. Wallace. Miss Rebecca and I had several lengthy discussions as to her will. She was quite insistent that everything, without exception, be left to you. I would encourage you to travel to Chambury as soon as possible; that's where her house as well as my office is located." Hearing no response from David, the man cleared his throat and continued.

"There is a great deal of paperwork to take care of

and I do believe it would be best not to leave the house unoccupied. As I mentioned, the house is located in the village of Chambury. That's in the county of Gloucestershire, in the southwest of England. Provide me with your email address and I'll send you the directions to Chambury and your aunt's house. That is, if you are indeed traveling here."

David took a deep breath. Until that moment he had been focused on leaving Scotland and returning to the States. The only thing that had stopped him was the faint and rapidly diminishing hope that Monica might return to him. Having now accepted that wasn't going to happen, an alternate plan suddenly formed in his mind. He would drive to Gloucestershire, take care of the paperwork, and then – as soon as humanly possible – sell the house. That should provide him more than enough for a flight to the States as well as the money necessary to start a new life. Best of all, it would get him as far away from his ex-wife and her lover as soon as possible. It was past time; David finally realized, to make a break with the past.

David gave the man his email address, thanked him for his call, and tapped the End Call icon on his mobile phone. Perhaps, he thought, his luck was changing. He then swallowed the eight-ounce glass of whiskey in two quick gulps.

#####

The email from Dylan Jones arrived less than an hour later. It repeated what the man had said during the phone call and ended with yet another strong recommendation that David should, just as soon as possible, travel to Chambury.

The email also provided detailed directions to Aunt Rebecca's house. Within minutes of the email's receipt, David had packed his meager belongings and placed them in the boot of his well traveled, ten year-old Renault Twingo. He could only hope that the car would make the nearly 500 mile trip to Chambury.

David made but one stop on his drive out of Aberdeen, and that was at a small grocery store and news agency located a block from his flat. The sign over the door read: *Wm. Robertson, News Agent,* but the store was actually owned and operated by a Pakistani named Abdul. David gave some serious thought to purchasing a chilled six-pack of Old Speckled Hen, his favorite beer, but, instead, simply picked up and paid for an AA Road Atlas of Britain.

Chapter 2

Chambury, Gloucestershire, England; Thursday, 15 April 2010: It had been a particularly dreary day. The light showers that had occurred earlier that morning had ceased but the sky remained overcast. It was, in fact, the type of day that encouraged one to stay indoors. Despite that, there were but three people in Chambury's public library. Two of those were employees: Liliana Kowalski, the 54 year-old head librarian, and her pretty, twenty-something assistant, Joyce Blake.

Twenty years ago the library would have been at least half full on a day like this. No longer. The dramatic decline in library patrons placed Liliana's sheltered existence under threat – a threat that had been put to voice in the previous evening's council meeting. The final item on the agenda of that meeting had seemed innocuous – yet another discussion of recommendations for improvements in the library's community service component. Quickly, however, the discussion had turned into a lightly veiled attack on Liliana's management skills.

Some of the council members actually recommended that the library be closed. Libraries, to them, were costly relics of an earlier time. A few, members of the *Keep Chambury Green Movement*, went so far as to assert that paper products of any kind, including books, were responsible for the deforestation of the planet and thus played a major role in climate change. Liliana's inquiry as to whether or not they felt the same way about toilet paper only served to amplify their displeasure.

The other half of the council, while in favor of maintaining the library, insisted that its services be expanded and modernized. They demanded the establishment of a tea and coffee kiosk, of playgroups for pre-schoolers, free Wi-Fi, and the rental of DVDs. And they insisted that the two existing computers that had been established almost a decade ago, for use by library patrons, be replaced by at least two dozen more up-to-date machines. Liliana's reply, that libraries were intended to serve as places of learning, not as taxpayer funded community centers, failed to resonate with her detractors.

Their displeasure was only increased when Liliana revealed her feelings with regard to the Internet. She ridiculed the growing reliance on the Internet for the search of anything and everything. She went so far as to say that those who relied on the Internet for information were both foolish and naïve. Even worse, in Liliana's opinion, was the growing trend of reading "eBooks."

Liliana Kowalski hated computers … and the Internet.

Liliana's unhappy reflections on the events of the previous evening vanished when she noticed the time. It was almost noon.

"Joyce," whispered Liliana as she stood up, "I'll be taking my lunch at the Fleming house. I'll be back about one and you can take your lunch then."

Joyce Blake nodded knowingly. Ever since the death of Rebecca Fleming, her superior had been "taking her lunch" at the Fleming house.

#####

Liliana's place of employment, the village's only library, was located at the very edge of the ancient and picturesque village of Chambury. The home of the late Rebecca Fleming was several blocks to the west, situated in what had once been a separate village but was now part of Chambury's pastoral suburbs.

Liliana, walking at her usual brisk pace, turned a corner. From that vantage point she could see Rebecca's house, as well as its surrounding stacked stone wall and the rustic gate leading to the front entrance of the attractive, two-story home. She could also see Molly's head poking out from the opening in the gate.

Molly, a five-year old yellow Labrador Retriever, had been Rebecca Fleming's pride and joy. She had showered her love and affection on the gentle animal: love and affection that were returned ten-fold. Molly had been in a kennel the week Rebecca died. She had remained in the kennel until Liliana fetched the dog, paid the kennel fees, and had taken Molly to her own lodgings – a small flat above an ironmonger's shop on Chambury's high street.

That had not worked out. Molly made several desperate escapes. Each time the dog was found in front of the gate that lead to her former mistress's house. Liliana finally gave up. She took the dog back to Rebecca's house. There it could either use a doggy-door to go inside or have the run of the front and back gardens.

Liliana tended to Molly's needs three times daily: once before work, once at noon, and then once each evening at which time she would place Molly, and the dog's favorite cuddly toy, in Molly's crate. During the day, Molly chose to spend the majority of her time standing behind the gate, head protruding through its opening, waiting in vain for the return of Rebecca.

Hopefully, thought Liliana, the new owner – the sole heir to Rebecca's estate – will allow Molly to remain at the one and only home the poor animal had ever known.

Molly backed away from the gate as Liliana approached. The woman opened the gate, patted Molly on the head, and walked to the entranceway of the house. She climbed the three steps leading to the door, opened her purse, retrieved a key, and inserted it into the keyhole. Turning to Molly, she said: "I'll be back in a minute, luv; just need to fetch your food and water."

#####

Reaching the kitchen, Liliana took a plate from a shelf over the kitchen sink and then opened the door of the fridge. She pulled out a tray from the vegetable compartment and removed an apple and a handful each of cut carrots and celery. That would serve, and had been serving for several weeks, as Liliana's lunch.

She then opened the door to the cupboard. It was empty except for a dozen or so cans of soup, a box of Weetabix, Molly's food dish, several bags of dog food, and, on the top shelf, a plush toy – a small teddy bear.

Returning to the front steps, Liliana placed the dish of dog food on the path leading to the gate. She then filled Molly's water dish from the house's hosepipe and placed it next to the food dish. Molly ignored her efforts and remained at the gate.

Liliana grasped Molly's collar and gently pulled her toward the food and water dishes. The dog took a few nibbles of dog food, lapped up some water, and then returned to her sentry duty at the gate.

"Molly, old girl, you need to understand that your mistress is not coming home ... ever. Oh, you poor, sweet dear, if only we could communicate."

At that very moment a slate grey Nissan Qashqai SUV stopped in front of the house. The driver's side door opened and Dylan Jones stepped out. Liliana, despite her attempt at self-control, felt an onslaught of bitterness building in her. She considered Dylan Jones to be a fraud, cheat, and liar, and rued the day that he had entered the life of her dear friend, Rebecca Fleming.

"Good day, Miss Kowalski," said Jones, a forced smile on his face.

"Hello, Mr. Jones. Any word as to the arrival of the new lord of the manor?"

Dylan ignored the sarcasm. "Yes, he emailed me a few minutes ago. He's having car trouble and won't be arriving until tomorrow afternoon. Poor chap says he'll be spending the night in some dodgy motel off the M5."

"Well," replied Liliana, "then I'd best stop by this evening and put Molly in her crate. That seems to be the only place the poor dear finds any peace anymore."

"No, no need to do that. I'll be by this evening. Please allow me to take care of things. I insist."

Although Dylan's words were polite, Liliana sensed

was actually ordering her not to return that
..ng. She nodded her head, picked up her plate
.d Molly's food dish, and returned them to the
kitchen. Dylan followed her into the house and then
gave her a perfunctory head nod as she passed him on
her way out.

Liliana was about to place her hand on the door
handle when Dylan had another request. "Miss
Kowalski, please leave your key to this house. I'll need
to give it to the new owner tomorrow. Do leave it on
the table by the door."

Liliana Kowalski hated Dylan Jones.

Dylan, standing behind a front room window,
watched the departure of Liliana. That the woman
disliked, perhaps even hated him, was all too obvious.
Liliana Kowalski wasn't someone who could hide her
feelings.

Dylan recalled the look on Liliana's face when he
had read Rebecca Fleming's will. Her expression had
changed, in a split second, from open mouth shock to
red-faced anger. The woman had been confident,
Dylan was sure, that she would inherit most if not all
of Rebecca's estate. Liliana had confronted Dylan
later that day, accusing him of turning Rebecca against
her.

Liliana Kowalski was, thought Dylan, an angry
woman. She was a woman who was full of rage. Had
it been enough rage, he wondered, to have actually
killed another human being?

Dylan Jones was still baffled by the circumstances
surrounding the death of Rebecca Fleming. The
elderly woman was bedridden and so weak that she

could hardly raise her head. How could she have, Dylan wondered, gathered enough strength to have left her bed, opened the door to the rear garden, and then walked some hundred or so meters to the pond where she had been found, face down and lifeless? The police may not have considered that odd but he found it truly extraordinary.

Dylan walked to the front door and looked for the spare key that he had asked Liliana to leave there. The table top was bare. Either the wretched woman hadn't heard him or had intentionally ignored him.

Chapter 3

M5 Motorway, England; Thursday, 15 April 2010: David left his ailing Renault Twingo at the garage. Its owner had advised him that the car, or motorcar as he insisted on calling it, was beyond saving. The man had, however, reluctantly agreed to do what he could to repair it to the degree necessary to, hopefully, travel the final 150 miles to his destination. But he made it clear that he would provide no guarantee.

Leaving the garage, David asked for directions to the nearest liquor store, purchased a bottle of its least expensive Scotch whisky, and walked to the seedy hotel at which he had booked the night. As soon as he reached his room he poured himself a drink. For a brief moment David wondered if he had become an alcoholic. Any concern about that vanished after his first sip.

As David lay in bed that night he made a mental review of the past year. The Queen may have had her "Annus horribilis" back in 1992, but he was quite sure that his year had been far more devastating. The Queen, and the Royal family, had recovered ... quite nicely. David wasn't sure that he ever would.

David Wallace was ... had been ... a safety engineer. It was his job to train and educate his fellow employees in the art and science of workplace safety. This included everything from an employee's posture at his or her computer console to the dangers involved in the operation of heavy, complex machinery. He was also skilled, according to his vita, in the identification and mitigation of potentially dangerous situations. A good safety engineer, he knew, should have an excellent memory, an ability to notice even minor changes in his or her surroundings, and the talent to sense and follow patterns.

An expert safety engineer should have, one of his professors had stated, something akin to the powers of observation and deduction exhibited by Sherlock Holmes, the fictional character created by Sir Arthur Conan Doyle. David Wallace was ... had been ... an excellent safety engineer.

David had received his degree, with honors, in engineering from a top-ranked university in America. Less than a year afterward he and his now ex-wife, Monica, had married.

Monica had been born and raised in Scotland and repeatedly encouraged David to find employment in her native country. Two years after tying the knot, David accepted a position with AXe, a major oil and gas exploration and production firm with offices in Aberdeen, Scotland. Although he had only moved to Scotland so as to satisfy his wife, he discovered that he enjoyed the work and, in particular, loved the country.

But not so much his boss.

David, as Head of Safety at AXe, reported to Simon Webb. Webb, some twenty years David's senior, was a blustering, bloviating man. Those two unpleasant characteristics were not, however, what most troubled David. Over the years it had become blindingly obvious that Webb was a weasel … taking credit for the accomplishments and achievements of others while blaming his subordinates for whatever might go wrong.

Six months ago something had gone terribly wrong at one of the firm's pumping stations. Simon Webb had previously, and repeatedly, overridden David's recommendations to replace two of its pumps. David had warned Webb that the seals on the pumps were defective and that the equipment should be replaced … immediately. If not, the pumping station should be shut down. Despite a flurry of emails and one heated, face-to-face meeting, Webb had ignored the warning. The senior management of AXe was obsessed with cost reduction, and Simon Webb was determined to please them.

Three days later one of the pumps failed, a fire was started, and an explosion followed. Four men were killed and twelve others seriously injured.

Simon Webb placed the blame squarely on David's shoulders. David was confident that the exchange of emails between himself and Webb would resolve that issue. Anyone reading that correspondence would have no doubt as to who had been the villain in the tragedy.

In the investigation that followed, however, it was determined that the emails between Webb and David were deemed "not recoverable." David's computer, that of Simon Webb, as well as anyone else that might have been privy to the emails concerning the defective pumps, had purportedly "crashed." The machines, their hard drives, and supposedly any other record of the emails were allegedly forever lost.

The only person who had actually heard a conversation between Webb and David, with regard to the situation, lied. The witness – a man David had considered a friend – claimed that David had never warned Webb as to the problems with the pumps and had, instead, ignored if not covered up the problem. The man, a man that David thought was a friend, received a promotion and substantial increase in salary a few days later.

David's employment was terminated. Shortly thereafter he discovered that his wife and his boss had been having an affair, one that had started some two years earlier. He also found out that his life savings had been looted. If that wasn't bad enough, David learned that he was a virtual *persona non grata* when he attempted to find employment in his field at other firms.

And so began David's love affair with alcohol … in any shape or form – and preferably cheap.

Chapter 4

Gloucestershire; Friday, 16 April 2010: The following morning David walked to the garage, paid its owner for the temporary, patchwork repairs, and headed south. As he entered the county of Gloucestershire, David could not help but notice the stark difference between that region and Scotland. Scotland and its windswept moors and mountains had reminded him of his birthplace, the rough and rugged Hill Country of central Texas. Everything had always seemed, somehow, bigger and wilder in either Scotland or Texas.

Gloucestershire, on the other hand, was tame, gentle, and extraordinarily beautiful. Its hedges, rolling hills, and picturesque villages seemed, to David, almost unnaturally neat. Its fields of green grass and wildflowers were in stark contrast to the heather encrusted hills of the Scottish Highlands. While he had loved Scotland, he felt that one could be quite happy in Gloucestershire.

#####

While the scenery was breath taking, the performance of the Twingo was unnerving. Frequent stops were required because of the car's overheating and, even when the water temperature gauge was within its redline limit, steering the car took every bit of strength that David could muster. Consequently, what should have been a three-hour drive took twice that long, and it was not until shortly after noon that David Wallace arrived at the outskirts of the town of Guyton-upon-Cham.

As instructed in Dylan Jones's directions, David found the narrow B-road that led from Guyton to Chambury. Turning onto that road, he drove its meandering five miles to the outskirts of Chambury. The first sign to meet him read: "Chambury: Bird Sanctuary." The second, about ten meters on, read: "Chambury, birthplace of Lord Reginald Emsworth." David could only wonder who "Lord Reginald Emsworth" was, and why the village was so proud of the man.

From what David could see, the modest sized village consisted mostly of stone buildings, none more than three stories high. The stones, he noted, were of a pale golden color rather than the slate grey, granite stones that characterized the buildings in Aberdeen. Chambury's high street was closed to motor vehicle traffic and thus David was forced to circle the village until he arrived at an intersection west of village center.

David pulled to the side of the road and used his mobile phone to check the directions to the house of Rebecca Fleming, the house that was now – at least according to a Mr. Dylan Jones – his. Retrieving the directions to the house, he noted that Jones had added a comment to the bottom of his email. It said "the house is situated on the south side of the street, at the corner of that street and a single-track road. There are neither signs nor house numbers but you'll most likely see a dog sticking her nose through the gate, a yellow Lab named Molly. Not to worry."

Following the directions, David found himself on a pleasant tree-shaded street. Up ahead he could see the head of a dog protruding through an opening in the top of a gate. The dog seemed to be looking for something … or someone. As David drove closer he was taken by the dog's eyes. They were, he was convinced, the most expressive – and saddest – eyes he had ever seen.

David parked his car behind a grey Nissan SUV. As he did, the front door of the house opened and a nattily dressed young man, probably in his late 20s or early 30s, appeared. He waved to David and then walked to the front gate of the house where he roughly seized the collar of the sad-eyed yellow Lab and brusquely shoved her aside.

If this is Dylan Jones, thought David, I'm not so sure I like him.

#####

Dylan Jones led David on a tour of the outside and interior of the Rebecca Fleming home. The style of the detached stone house was early Victorian. David's initial impression was that it was a well-built, solid structure with no apparent problems. The roof was slate and appeared, to David's eyes, to be in excellent condition. The front and back gardens were well tended and quite lovely. David was particularly impressed with the rear garden's hydrangeas as well as a lovely shrub abloom with fragrant, pale yellow flowers.

The interior of the house was equally impressive. While the furnishings appeared to be relics of the Edwardian era, they were in good condition and could probably be sold for a decent price at an estate sale. The only negative was the smell; the inside of the house smelled like a mix of lavender and mothballs. That should not present a problem, thought David, that a good airing out of the house couldn't fix.

David was convinced that Aunt Rebecca's house should be an easy sell. Dylan Jones was of a rather different opinion.

"The house is more than 150 years old and has seen better days," said Dylan. "I'm afraid that its heating system is on its last legs. And don't expect to use any of its fireplaces unless you invest in some much-needed repairs and a thorough chimney cleaning. You wouldn't want a chimney fire to burn the house down.

"Then there's the plumbing. In a word, the plumbing is in horrid shape and I'm surprised the house has survived this long without suffering major water damage. Yes, the house looks fine, even quite attractive on the surface but, as they say, beauty is only skin deep."

David decided not to argue. All that he wanted to do was to sell the house, whatever its real or imagined condition, just as soon as possible.

Dylan Jones was not, however, finished with his bleak assessment of the house. "I should also warn you that you will be facing some quite high taxes. In fact, there will be a substantial inheritance tax – along what will likely seem to be a never ending list of fees."

"An inheritance tax?" asked David, realizing that was something he had not factored into his plan.

"Definitely; as executor of the will it is my responsibility to pay that tax. Of course, I won't be paying it out of my own funds; instead those monies must come from the estate. Unfortunately, for you, Miss Rebecca has only about three thousand pounds in her savings – not nearly enough to cover the inheritance tax. You, as the heir, will have to cover the bulk of that tax – plus any fees."

David shook his head. "Mr. Jones, that's only going to be possible if the tax and fees amount to less than what I've got in my wallet. When I last checked I have a total of 92 pounds and six pence."

Dylan Jones's eyes narrowed. "Then, Mr. Wallace, we … you … have a problem."

"What if we simply sell the house and everything else I've inherited and use the proceeds to pay off the taxes and fees?"

"Sorry, but the house must be free and clear of any encumbrances before it can be put up for sale. That's a nasty little restriction the district council imposed a few years back."

"Damn," said David, "I wish you would have told me all of this before I drove here. It looks like this has all been one big waste of time."

"Not necessarily. There is a way to resolve the issue. There's a potential buyer, a buyer who is *very* interested in the house and who, I'm convinced, will pay top dollar. Frankly, he seems to have an emotional attachment to the place for some reason or another.

"Mr. Wallace, I can loan you the funds necessary to cover the taxes and fees and, just as soon as the house is sold, you can pay me back, plus, of course, a small fee. Once the taxes and fees have been paid the house will be yours free and clear and you are then free to sell it. That will be a way for you to make a modest profit on the house and a means for me to gain the goodwill of the purchaser."

"I suppose that's my only alternative," said David. "I truly appreciate your offer to help. But, please, let me have some time to think this over."

"Well, it's Friday. Do you believe that you could come to a decision by, say, Monday morning? In the meantime, feel free to take your accommodations here. Miss Rebecca's bedroom is on this level and there are two nicely furnished guestrooms upstairs. Choose whichever of the three you want. After all, very soon this will all be legally yours."

David Wallace had, as a consequence of the disastrous past several months, lost much of his naiveté. In fact, his faith in his fellow humans had decreased to something well below zero. Upon Dylan Jones's departure, David conducted a thorough inspection of Rebecca Fleming's home. Other than a few extremely minor matters – two leaky taps, a cooker that would need replacing, and a front gate that needed some minor repairs – he found nothing of substance wrong with the house or the grounds. Instead, he was convinced that the house was in remarkably good condition and appeared to have been exceptionally well maintained. Dylan Jones, he suspected, was being less than honest with him.

David then took another look at the grounds. They were quite lovely, particularly those in the back garden. Its two magnolia trees, hydrangeas, and rhododendrons were all in bloom – as was the unusual shrub – with its yellow, star-shaped flowers –

planted near the garden shed. The plants were in excellent condition and several appeared to have been recently trimmed and pruned. David wondered just who took care of the grounds. He rather doubted that it had been his elderly great aunt.

Finishing his inspection of the house and its gardens, David decided to prepare himself a late dinner. He opened the cupboard and discovered that its only contents were several bags of dog food, what appeared to be a dog dish, four large bags of crisps, and – at eye level on its top shelf – six bottles of whiskey: McIvor Scotch whiskey to be precise. Opening the fridge, he found that its sole contents were a dozen bottles of beer: Old Speckled Hen pale ale. It appears, thought David, that his late Aunt Rebecca must have existed on a liquid diet – a diet astonishingly similar to the one he had become accustomed to over the past several months. As he contemplated the contents of the fridge he heard a sharp knock on the front door.

The late night caller was a woman – a short, plain, and rather severe looking woman. She introduced herself as Liliana Kowalski, a close friend of David's late great aunt.

"I was driving by and saw Molly, your aunt's dog," said Liliana, "at the front gate. She's normally in the house at this time of night. The poor dear's crate-trained and always spends the night in her crate. Dylan Jones – whom I assume you've met – had promised me that he'd take care to tell you to place Molly in her crate each evening."

"Mr. Jones didn't mention anything about that," said David, sensing a growing dislike of Dylan Jones.

"How does one go about enticing Molly to come in?"

Liliana walked to the gate, took hold of Molly's collar, and gently led the dog into the house. "Her crate is in the small room off the rear entrance," said Liliana. "Molly is still grieving for Rebecca, but as long as you place her in the crate along with her favorite cuddly toy, she'll have a peaceful night. As will you."

As Liliana passed through the kitchen she opened the door to the cupboard. "My word, Molly's little teddy bear seems to be missing. Mr. Wallace, you wouldn't have happened to have replaced Molly's cuddly toy with what would appear to be at least a six months' supply of whiskey, would you?"

"I haven't seen any cuddly toy and had assumed that the whiskey in the cupboard, along with the dozen bottles of beer in the fridge, had been placed there by my aunt. It most certainly isn't mine."

"Your aunt never touched alcohol. Furthermore, none of this," said Liliana, pointing to the contents of the third shelf, "was here when I fed Molly at noon yesterday. Nor was there anything in the fridge but some vegetables and a few apples, and they seem to have been replaced with beer."

"Miss Kowalski, I think we should talk," said David. "Would you care to have a seat in the drawing room?"

"Yes, that might be a good idea. But first allow me to make us some tea," said Liliana, eyeing the silver serving tray and its tea set on the kitchen counter. "Do take a seat in the drawing room and I'll be right with you."

As David left the kitchen, Liliana removed her windbreaker and placed it on the back of a kitchen chair. She then examined the contents of the sugar and creamer set. The cream had gone bad and, raising the top to the sugar bowl, she found it was empty. Well, not completely empty as there was a powdery residue on the bottom of the bowl.

Liliana eyed the sugar bowl, frowned, gave the matter some thought, and then placed the bowl in the pocket of her windbreaker. The only witness to that odd event was a sad-eyed yellow Lab.

"Come, Molly," said Liliana as she left the kitchen and headed toward the drawing room.

#####

"I'm afraid we'll have to pass on the tea; there's neither cream nor sugar. One simply cannot have tea without, at the very least, cream," said Liliana as she took a seat in the drawing room.

"That's quite all right. I'm not much of a tea drinker anyhow." David paused for a moment and then got to the point. "Miss Kowalski, what's your opinion as to the condition of this house? Did my aunt mention having problems with the house? Its plumbing? Electrical system?"

Liliana was still struggling to comprehend just how and why Rebecca's cupboard and fridge were filled with liquor when the man, the tall Yank, had suddenly asked a rather odd question. Before attempting to answer, she studied David Wallace. The man was good looking, not quite movie star handsome but still rather attractive.

Unlike most Americans she had met, he was neither loud nor pushy. Instead he was soft spoken and polite. She was concerned, however, by the fact that he was now asking her some rather odd questions, or at least questions that seemed out-of-place.

"The house, as far as I know, is in excellent condition. Your aunt came into some money about four or five years ago and spent a considerable amount on the maintenance of her house – a new roof, some rewiring, and virtually anything else she believed needed repair. As I said, as far as I'm aware, the house is in remarkably good shape for its age."

"You say she came into money? I was under the assumption that she had but a small amount of funds in a savings account."

"I was never privy to your aunt's finances, and I really have no idea as to the source of her good fortune. We were close but money was not something I ever recall discussing with her. I do know that she was, at least until a few years ago, a keen reader of financial newspapers and books on investing. That, in fact, is how we first met some twenty-five years ago. I had just accepted employment at our village's library and your aunt had just moved here. Rebecca dropped by nearly every morning and spent hours reading the financial newspapers and newsletters. She would also borrow books on finance and investing. Her interest in that, however, changed a few years ago. She suddenly became a voracious reader of romance novels."

"Romance novels," said David, shaking his head. "Just how old was Aunt Rebecca?"

"Your aunt was 84 when she passed away and, by the way, a woman is never too old for romance novels."

David, now blushing, attempted to change the

subject. "What did my aunt die from? Old age?"

"Up until a week or so before her death, I don't believe your aunt had ever been sick a day in her life. Every morning she and Molly would walk the mile or so into the village, and then continue another half mile or more up High Street. You could set your clocks by those two. Rebecca fell sick, however, soon after returning from a trip to the continent. Her doctor couldn't find anything wrong with her; she just became weaker and weaker."

"Oh," said David, "so she died in her bed?"

"No, she drowned."

"Drowned! My God, how on earth does a bedridden octogenarian drown?"

"About a week after falling ill she was found in the pond – the very one behind this house. She was lying, face down, in the pond. Evidently she drowned in less than a foot of water."

"That's terribly odd," said David.

"That's what I thought," Liliana replied. "There was, however, an autopsy. They found water in her lungs and so it was shown that she had indeed drowned. She had to have been alive when she fell into the pond. Case closed, at least according to the local authorities."

#####

Liliana left soon after her disclosure as to the circumstances of Rebecca Fleming's death. David drew the curtains to the drawing room windows and walked into the kitchen. He went to the fridge and removed the twelve bottles of beer. He then opened each bottle and poured the contents into the sink. He repeated that act with the six bottles of whiskey.

David had come to the conclusion that Dylan Jones had placed the liquor in the fridge and cupboard. The man had also lied to him about the condition of the house. David intended to be cold sober when he next met the lying Mr. Jones.

After placing the empty bottles in the rubbish bin, David happened to glance at the tea set on the kitchen counter. There, he realized, a piece missing. The sugar bowl had disappeared – along with the departure of Liliana Kowalski, village librarian.

David had only been in Chambury a matter of hours and had only met two of its inhabitants. One, he strongly suspected, was a liar. The other was quite possibly a liar – and most definitely a thief.

David was to discover that at least one thing Liliana Kowalski had told him was true. Molly would not go to sleep without the missing cuddly toy. The dog cried, a soft moaning whimper that was heart breaking to hear, until David opened the crate.

To keep Molly from venturing outside during the night, David placed an armchair in front of the doggy door. Hopefully, he thought, that will keep the dog inside for the night and stop her crying. That seemed to work, although it produced an unexpected result. Wherever David would walk in the house, Molly followed. When he took a seat on a drawing room armchair, the dog lay on the rug in front of the fireplace, never taking her eyes off David.

When David decided to go to bed, in what he had been told was an upstairs guest bedroom, Molly followed him. She lay in the open doorway, watching him as he prepared to retire for the night. She was still there, and still watching, when David turned off the lights.

Sometime later that night David woke to discover that Molly was now on top of the bed, sleeping soundly next to him. He was evidently serving as a suitable replacement for her cuddly toy.

Chapter 5

Cheltenham, England; Saturday, 17 April 2010: Although Mildred Pankhurst had gone to bed early, it was now half-past two in the morning and she was wide-awake. Rupert, her bedfellow, had been having a bad night. Mildred rolled to her left side to check once more on him. The poor dear had finally fallen asleep, his breathing no longer labored. The pain pill she had given him at midnight had finally soothed him.

Mildred felt guilty about what she had put Rupert through. It must be quite traumatic for a male to have his testicles removed. She shuddered whenever she thought about it. But Rupert had been unable to resist the feminine wiles of his attractive next door neighbor and had left Mildred with no choice but to have him neutered.

Mildred decided that she would try to make it up to him, perhaps buy him a new toy, or a bigger and better scratching post. And she would definitely refresh his supply of catnip.

Her concern for her cat somewhat alleviated, Mildred focused her thoughts on another matter – that of a partially completed manuscript she had received over a month ago. Its author was a young woman named Catherine Cromwell. Mildred was convinced that Catherine was a rising star, a woman destined to best seller status in the increasingly crowded world of romance novelists. Catherine Cromwell, she believed, could well become the Barbara Cartland of the 21st century. Or, at the very least, yet another Penny Jordan. Catherine Cromwell had a "gift."

But the latest manuscript that Catherine had sent her could not be considered to be, by any stretch of the imagination, a romance novel. While it was an exceptionally well-crafted and fascinating tale of heartbreak, betrayal, and undying love, it did not appear that it would have the happy ending required of any marketable romance novel. As Mildred had advised Catherine Cromwell several years ago, the formula *de rigueur* for a *successful* romance novel is the inclusion of six essential ingredients:

* a young, relatively inexperienced girl
* a handsome, mysterious, yet vulnerable man a few years older than the girl
* a sweet, blossoming romance
* a misunderstanding that threatens the romance
* a resolution of the misunderstanding
* a happy ending

One thing that Mildred had learned, in her years as a literary agent, was that any aspiring romance novelist who ignored that formula did so at her own peril. Catherine Cromwell – to her credit – had followed that formula, to the letter, in her previous seven romance novels. Her first work had sold modestly well. Those that followed had each performed better and better and, by her seventh novel, she had attracted a relatively large and admiring audience. Mildred had been confident that Catherine's eighth novel, still in the draft stage, would be a breakout success – the novel that could well make Catherine Cromwell a household word. And yet Catherine had left that work unfinished, to pursue a novel she had tentatively titled: *Obsession.*

Obsession, at least what Mildred had read thus far, exhibited writing skills that were a quantum leap above and beyond those Catherine had exhibited in her previous works, but it simply was not a romance novel. Mildred Pankhurst had never represented anyone other than romance novelists.

Romance novels, along with cozy mysteries, formed the basis for the success – modest though it may have been – of the Passionate Word Literary Agency. Mildred, as the most junior partner in that agency, depended upon the commissions on the royalties of the authors she represented. She was at a loss as to how to convince Catherine Cromwell to return to her unfinished romance novel and abandon *Obsession.*

Mildred realized, however, that one reason for her own reluctance to encourage the writing of *Obsession* was a selfish concern for her own well being. Mildred had spent much of the past month in hospital. She had been assured that the removal of her appendix would be a simple matter. That had been true until she contracted an infection. Only now, some four weeks later, was she able to return home and proceed with her life and chosen career.

Fiona Branch, owner of the Passionate Word Literary Agency, had warned Mildred against even considering the representation of any authors other than those writing romance novels. She had made a convincing argument. Survey after survey show that adult women read more novels than men, attend more book clubs than men, and buy more books than men – and these women make up approximately 80 per cent of the readers of fiction. Furthermore, the most popular genre read by these women is the romance novel. So, according to Fiona, Mildred should not waste her time, and the agency's resources, on anything other than romance novels.

#####

Unable to sleep, Mildred decided to get up and brew herself a cup of tea. Tip-toeing out of the bedroom so as to not wake Rupert, she walked the few steps to the tiny kitchen of her living quarters – a small, second level flat in the town of Cheltenham and a short walk to her place of employment.

As she sat at the kitchen table, sipping her tea, Mildred attempted to devise a plan, a plan that would allow her to talk, face-to-face, with Catherine Cromwell. Although the woman lived less than fifty miles from Cheltenham, she had – time and time again – refused to meet with Mildred. Their *only* mode of communication had been via the post. Mildred received hand-written letters and typewritten manuscripts and replied to the only address she had for the woman: a mail stop in the village of Chambury.

Catherine Cromwell, while a gifted writer, was a difficult client. She had insisted upon using a financial services firm as a go-between for all monetary and legal matters. All royalties, less the agency's commissions, had to be deposited in an account held by that firm.

The woman eschewed communication by phone.

She refused to use email and, instead, employed what seemed to be an old, manual typewriter to write her manuscripts.

Catherine Cromwell seemed intent on breaking all the rules and ignoring all the conventional wisdom upon which the promotion and marketing of books had been founded. The woman even refused to establish a social media presence – no Facebook, Twitter, or blogs for the obstinate Catherine. Nor any book signings, radio or television appearances, or book tours. The only personal detail that Mildred knew about Catherine Cromwell was what she looked like – having been sent a photograph of the young woman – and her mailbox rental store address and box number.

Halfway through her tea, Mildred had an idea. *If the mountain will not come to Mahomet, Mahomet must go to the mountain.*

Chapter 6

Chambury, England; Saturday, 17 April 2010: Detective Constable Thomasina Blake, known to her friends and co-workers as "Tommi," tip-toed past her sister's room. She was wearing civilian clothes, a brand new business suit purchased just last week from the Austin Reed store in Cheltenham. The suit had cost her nearly a week's salary but today was a special day.

It was at least 15 minutes till sunrise but the 29 year-old wanted to make sure that she was at HQ in Guyton-upon-Cham before the arrival of Detective Chief Inspector Keith Grahame. While Guyton-upon-Cham lay but five miles distant, the narrow road between it and Chambury was, to say the least, a bit tricky and required a minimum drive time of 15 minutes.

DCI Grahame was being transferred from his previous post in London and Tommi had been informed, only three days ago, that she would be serving, at least informally, as his "assistant." Tommi had never met the man and was both concerned and perplexed by the rumors that had been spread about him.

Some said that DCI Grahame was a superb detective with a keen mind and long record of having solved some very complex and difficult crimes. His transfer to Guyton-upon-Cham, they asserted, had been initiated because of the severe and worsening understaffing of the station.

Others claimed that he was being transferred to Guyton as a punishment. They believed the rumors that implied that Keith Grahame had gone mental, that he had badly botched an important case, and that London was simply dumping its rubbish in Guyton.

Grahame had also recently acquired, so rumors claimed, an odd habit. He often wore, it was said, tinted glasses. The man supposedly claimed that the glasses allowed him to more carefully appraise a person, particularly a suspect being interrogated. The suspect could not see Grahame's eyes, a factor that – so claimed the DCI – made the person even more uncomfortable than under normal circumstances and thus led to faster confessions.

Other rumors claimed that DCI Grahame simply did not want his fellow workers to readily observe the pupils of his eyes. Grahame, some believed, had become an addict. Tommi dismissed that rumor immediately, unable to believe that the man could retain the position of DCI and be taking drugs. Such a person, she believed, would certainly be found out.

Guyton-upon-Cham; Saturday, 17 April 2010: Tommi Blake arrived at HQ in Guyton-upon-Cham a few minutes before 6 a.m. DCI Grahame had arrived, according to PC Billy Milne, a full hour earlier – and wanted to see her. The man was sitting in his office, wearing a pair of tinted glasses and examining a record of recent calls.

Tommi tapped on the window to the door of Grahame's office. The man didn't look up from his reading and simply beckoned for her to enter.

"Sir," said Tommi, standing in front of the DCI's desk, "I'm DC Blake …'

Grahame interrupted. "Blake, I'm told that you know this district well." The man then placed the call sheet face down on his desk and, for the first time, raised his head and actually looked at her. The man's tinted glasses failed to conceal his surprise.

"My word; how tall are you, Blake?"

Tommi didn't like the question, but she answered her superior. "Exactly 1.8 meters, Sir, a wee bit under 6 feet."

Keith Grahame eyed the woman, DC Tommi Blake, from behind his tinted eyeglasses. She looked, he thought, like an Amazon. She was not only tall, considerably taller than him, but she also had the build and posture of an athlete. "You do sports, Blake?"

"Rowing, archery, and lacrosse, sir."

The woman, thought Grahame, could be attractive but wore little if any makeup. Hopefully that was a good sign. "I understand that you are a local … Blake, do have a seat."

Tommi sat down before answering Grahame's question. "Sir, I was born and raised in the village of Chambury. It's about five miles from here. My sister and I live there; she works at the village library."

DCI Grahame took his time digesting that response. Tommi took advantage of that pause to further appraise the man. Even though he was sitting, she guessed he was several inches shorter than her. He had a stocky build and a short, thick neck. Based on his build, his large hands, and a nose that had likely been broken more than once, Tommi guessed he had either been a rugby player or a boxer at some time in his life.

"Blake, I want you in uniform from now on," said Grahame, removing his glasses. "No need to change from your civilian clothes just now, but from hereon, please do wear your uniform."

Tommi, not quite believing what she had just heard, nodded her head in reply.

"But for now, let's take a drive," said Grahame. "I want you to give me the guided tour. Oh, and what the hell's a 'volvo?' There's a report on the call sheet about a pub fight where someone tossed a 'volvo' in another person's face. Either the drunks around here are awfully strong or this particular 'volvo' isn't a car."

"It would be a drink, sir. A 'volvo' is a drink consisting of vodka and coke. It's an Irish term. There was a fight last night in McCarthy's pub and I imagine PC Nolan used the term in his report; he's Irish – or at least his parents are."

"Let Nolan know that he's to use the Queen's English from now on."

Chapter 7

Chambury; Saturday, 17 April 2010: David woke to a strange sensation. Something … or someone … was tugging on his bedcovers. Opening his eyes, he saw that the someone was Molly. The sad-eyed dog didn't bark but she certainly made her feelings clear – she wanted David up and out of bed.

"Take it easy, Molly, I'm up. Easy girl," said David as he swung his legs over the edge of the bed.

With Molly leading the way, David hurried down the stairs and into the kitchen, thinking that Molly wanted to be fed. Instead, the dog nudged David toward the rear of the house and then to the doggy door that he had blocked with a chair the evening before. David moved the chair and Molly hurried out. Standing at a window, he watched as Molly made a dash through the back garden, and then up and over a grassy knoll some fifty meters or so to the rear of the house. David walked to the kitchen, opened the cupboard doors, and poured a generous helping of dog food into Molly's food dish.

David decided that, since there was nothing for him to eat in the house but bags of crisps, he would shower, get dressed, and walk into village center. There must certainly be a place to order breakfast there.

Having shaved and showered, David was in the

process of tying his shoes when Molly appeared at the door of the bedroom. She had something in her mouth: a leash and collar. The clever canine made it clear that she was expecting David to take her for a walk.

"Molly, old girl, I do believe that you can say more with one look than any politician can say in a two hour-long speech. And, I might add, a whole lot more convincingly. All right, Molly, let's go for a walk."

Molly dropped the leash and collar at David's feet. Picking them up, David noticed that the collar was different from the one Molly was wearing. It was of a much finer leather and there was a small metal container attached to it. Opening the container, David discovered that it held a key. The key, in turn, had a number engraved on it. Other than that, there was no indication as to what the key might fit. David put the key in his pocket and then placed the collar on Molly.

#####

They had walked less than two blocks before David realized that he wasn't taking Molly for a morning stroll. Instead the dog was leading him.

When they reached the edge of the village, Molly stopped in front of a butcher shop. As she sat back on her haunches it was clear that she was waiting for something to happen.

"Molly, dear girl, by God it's good to see you this fine morning," bellowed a voice from inside the shop. A short, heavyset man, dressed in traditional English butcher's regalia, a navy-stripped apron and white trilby hat, appeared at the door of the shop.

"Ah," said the man, eyeing David, "you must be the Yank, Miss Fleming's nephew what inherited her place. Welcome to our village," he added, extending his hand, "I'm Frank Owen, by the way."

"I'm David Wallace; pleased to meet you Mr. Owen. Seems as if you and Molly, here, are well acquainted."

"Most certainly," said Frank Owen, "Molly and your dear aunt dropped by my shop almost every day … until, of course Miss Fleming took ill. Terribly sorry about that."

The butcher reached into a jar next to the open door and retrieved a dog biscuit. Molly never moved from her sitting position but did shift her attention to David.

"I believe Molly's asking for your permission," said the butcher. "Miss Fleming taught her to never take any food or treats without permission. Why don't you try saying 'yes' to her? That worked for Miss Fleming."

"Yes," said David, looking into Molly's eyes. The dog immediately rose from the sitting position and retrieved the biscuit.

"Good girl," said Frank Owen. Turning his attention to David, he said: "When you've finished the circuit, Molly will most likely lead you back here. Miss Fleming oftentimes finished her circuit with the purchase of a half-dozen of my bangers."

"Circuit?" asked David. "What 'circuit' are you referring to?"

"Molly and Miss Fleming always – well, almost always – made the same stops on their walk. "I'm not a betting man but, if I were, I'd bet that your next stop is going to be six stores up. Just follow Molly."

#####

Six stores up the street, and just as Frank Owen had predicted, Molly stopped in front of a storefront. The sign on the window read: *One-Stop Shop for your Printing & Copying, Packaging, and Mail Address.* A smaller sign on the shop's door warned that dogs were NOT allowed inside.

David wondered just why his aunt and Molly might want to stop in front of such a store. Then he recalled the key he had placed in his pocket.

David wrapped Molly's leash around a metal pole directly in front of the shop. "I'll be right back, Molly. Stay here, I'll be right back."

The store was empty except for one employee, possibly the shop's owner. The man glanced at David, then – without a word of welcome – turned his back on him.

"Make sure that dog stays outside," said the man – his back still turned to David.

David didn't reply. Instead he walked to a long bank of mailboxes. Finding one whose number matched that on the key he had found on Molly's collar, he opened the box. Inside were six envelopes. Four – including one quite thick manila envelope – were addressed to a "Miss Catherine Cromwell." The other two were addressed to Rebecca Fleming.

David placed all but the manila envelope in the inside pocket of his jacket. Holding the larger item of correspondence in his hand, he closed the door to the mailbox. Once outside he untied Molly's leash from the metal pole and allowed her to lead him to the next stop on her "circuit."

That next stop was a bakery. The two women inside were delighted to see Molly. After exchanging pleasantries, David purchased a cup of coffee, a cinnamon bun, and two loaves of hot-from-the-oven wheat bread. He then took a table next to a window where he intended to have the coffee and bun for breakfast. First, however, he placed the large manila envelope on the table and removed the six letters from his jacket pocket.

All of the correspondence addressed to "Miss Catherine Cromwell" was from the Passionate Word Literary Agency, evidently located in Cheltenham. The two that had been sent to "Rebecca Fleming" were from a financial advisory service, Dorrit and Dombey, also located in Cheltenham.

As David sipped his coffee, he stared at the envelopes. They were certainly not meant for him, and he had no idea who "Catherine Cromwell" might be, but ... damn it ... they were in his aunt's mailbox and he was sole heir to her estate. Having convinced himself that he had a right to find out what was in the letters, he opened one of those addressed to Catherine Cromwell – the one with the most recent posting date.

The letter was from a Mildred Pankhurst. Based on the woman's name, David envisioned its writer as a bespectacled dowager, possibly a former school chum of his late aunt. But then, why was it addressed to "Catherine Cromwell?"

Mildred Pankhurst was asking, more like begging, Catherine Cromwell to finish a manuscript, a manuscript titled: *A Cotswold Diary*. She pleaded with Catherine to focus on her "romance novel" and to not let the writing of *Obsession* divert her from the completion of *A Cotswold Diary*. Mildred concluded her letter with yet another plea: to consider the use of a computer to write her novels as well as to consider communication by means of phone or email.

Wondering if the thick manila envelope might contain the draft of a novel, David opened it. Inside, as he had suspected, was a typewritten manuscript. It was indeed titled *A Cotswold Diary*. Someone, evidently Mildred Pankhurst, had critiqued it as there were some proof-reader's marks on several pages. On the very last page of the unfinished manuscript was yet another plea from Mildred. She had written, in longhand, a note that read: "Catherine, this is excellent. You've written a real page turner. I really do believe we can sell the movie rights to this work. Please, please, finish this book before even considering any further effort on *Obsession*."

David placed the manuscript back in its envelope and decided to open one of the letters from the financial services firm. It contained a financial statement, listing a brokerage account balance – in the name of Rebecca Fleming – in the amount of 323,186 pounds sterling!

He quickly opened the other letter from the financial services firm. It was a listing of deposits to the account of Miss Rebecca Fleming for the most recent quarter. There was but one deposit. It was for 11,452 pounds. It was cited as having been received from PASWRD AGCY.

David stared at the entry for a minute or so and then guessed that PASWRD AGCY was most likely an abbreviation for the Passionate Word Literary Agency. Aunt Rebecca had evidently received a quarterly royalty payment in the amount of 11,452 pounds from that agency – the very same agency that had sent four letters and an unfinished manuscript to a "Catherine Cromwell."

Clearly, thought David, his late aunt had far more than the three thousand or so pounds that Dylan Jones had claimed. Was the man lying about her money as well as the condition of her house? Or could it be that he simply did not know about the brokerage account?

#####

The remainder of Molly's "circuit" consisted of a stop at a green grocer's shop, where David purchased some fruit, and a return to the first stop on the tour: the butcher shop. On the advice of Frank Owen, the shop owner, he purchased a half-dozen bangers and 300 grams of bacon.

Returning to the Fleming house, David placed the two loaves of bread and the fruit in the cupboard and put the bangers and bacon in the fridge. Molly then led him into the small room in the rear of the house. In America it would probably be called a "mud room." The room contained a small bench, a nearly new Samsung ecobubble washer-dryer combination, and several rows of shelves on its far wall.

David sat down on the bench and removed Molly's collar and leash. She picked both up in her teeth and headed straight for the row of shelves where she attempted to place the equipment on the bottom-most shelf. Molly seemed, however, to be having some difficulty with the placement of the leash.

David walked over to the shelves and attempted to push the leash farther back on the shelf. He felt some resistance; there was something in the back of the shelf that was blocking any effort to neatly fit the leash and collar. He then removed the leash and collar and reached into the shelf. The "something" that had been blocking the shelf was a large manila envelope.

David removed the large envelope, thinking that it might be another Catherine Cromwell manuscript from the Passionate Word Literary agency. There were, however, no markings whatsoever on the outside of the envelope nor was it nearly as thick as had been the envelope containing *A Cotswold Diary*. Opening it, he found that it contained a number of what appeared to be newspaper clippings. Most were yellow with age and appeared to have been cut from foreign newspapers. His best guess was that they were from Polish newspapers as the word, "Polska," seemed to appear frequently.

With Molly following close behind, David walked upstairs to the room that evidently served as his late aunt's office. It contained a large desk, an impressive leather swivel chair, rows of book shelves, and three file cabinets. Sitting prominently on the surface of the desk was a vintage Underwood model SX-150 manual typewriter, circa 1950.

David placed the envelope he had retrieved from the mud room on the desktop. Then, after adjusting the height of the swivel chair, he opened the envelope once again and placed its contents on the top of the desk. Scanning the newspaper clippings, he found that, while most were evidently written in Polish, several were from English papers. Some of the clippings were recent while others were yellow and faded with age.

One of the items in the envelope was not, however, a newspaper clipping. Instead it was a receipt from a car hire company, a firm located at the John Paul II International Airport in Krakow, Poland. Evidently Aunt Rebecca had hired both a car and driver in Krakow and, according to the date on the receipt, that had been roughly three weeks ago.

What on earth, thought David, was his 84 year-old aunt doing in Poland? And just what was the significance of the newspaper clippings? While he might never unravel that mystery, there was another one that appeared to have an easy answer. That was the mystery of the typewritten manuscript and letters from the Passionate Word Literary Agency that had been found in his late aunt's mailbox.

David guessed that the manuscript, *A Cotswold Diary*, had been written on the antique typewriter sitting before him. He intended to compare the typing on the manuscript with that of the old Underwood but, before doing that, he noticed a row of paperback books sitting prominently on the top shelf of the bookcase to his left. If he was not mistaken, the author's name on each was Catherine Cromwell.

There were, he discovered, two copies each of seven different "Catherine Cromwell" romance novels on the shelf. David examined the front cover of one of the paperbacks. It was the stereotypical romance novel cover, featuring a swooning, ample bosomed young woman embracing a handsome, shirtless young man. In the background was either a castle or stately home. The book's title was *The Savage Earl*.

The back cover provided a blurb for the story. Underneath that was the photograph of the author, an exceptionally beautiful young woman. The name under the picture was that of Catherine Cromwell.

David, hands now shaking, stared in wonder at the picture. He knew the woman in the photo; it was his mother, Ann Wallace. He may have been only seven when his mother died, but there was no doubt in his mind. The picture on the back cover was his mother, as was the photo on the back of all the "Catherine Cromwell" romance novels on the shelf.

There was, he realized, no need to compare the printing of the manual typewriter on his aunt's desk with that on the manuscript. Rebecca Fleming and Catherine Cromwell were one and the same person.

David took a seat on the office chair; he needed some time to comprehend what he had discovered that morning.

Chapter 8

Lord Emsworth's Manor House, Chambury; Saturday, 17 April 2010: Lord Emsworth was not amused. "You want me to loan you 100 thousand pounds? Are you barking mad?"

"But your lordship," Dylan Jones replied, "the money is needed to pay off the taxes and fees on the house. That has to be done before it can be sold. The Yank, as I informed you previously, is penniless as well as a drunk. I'll need to provide him with the funds necessary to unencumber the house and, as soon as it is in his name, it's yours to purchase. I can assure you that he'll sell it to you as soon as the paperwork is completed."

"Bloody hell," replied Lord Emsworth, "bloody bleeding hell. All right, Jones, you'll have the money Monday; Tuesday at the latest. Just get moving on this thing. I'll be ninety next month, man! I want my bloody house back before I die."

"Your lordship, I can promise you that the house will be yours by the end of next week. The Yank's desperate for money and anxious to get back to the States."

Lord Emsworth's son, Henry, had been listening in silence to the exchange. He caught his father's eye and, like a timid child, raised his hand.

"Go ahead, Henry, what do you have to say?" said

Lord Emsworth impatiently.

"I want to know more about this Yank," asked Henry, his eyes now focused on Dylan Jones. "What's he like? All you've said so far is that he's a drunk and nearly destitute."

"He's your typical cowboy Yank," Dylan Jones replied. "Looks a bit like a young Clint Eastwood. Has a Texas drawl. I understand that he was even a rodeo bull rider for a while ... at least until he had his back broken and decided to attend university."

"Anything else?" asked Henry, his brow furrowed.

"Well, his automobile is on its last legs. He's got it parked in front of the house. The man left Aberdeen without paying his last two months' rent. Oh, yeah, he likes McIvor Scotch whiskey and has been falling down drunk every night for the past few months. I suppose ..."

Lord Emsworth interrupted. "That's quite enough, Jones. Just take care of this matter as soon as possible."

"Father wants to die in the house he was born in," said Henry.

"Henry, ring Wooster and have him show Jones the door," said Lord Emsworth as he gripped the brake release on his wheelchair.

Dylan Jones left the study and scurried to the massive door of the entrance of Emsworth's stately home. Wooster, Emsworth's insufferable butler, was already at the door, holding it open for Jones's departure. Dylan ignored the smirk on the man's face as he hurried out of the house and to his car.

Dylan got into his SUV and drove down the wide lane

that led to and from Lord Emsworth's stately home. Dylan did not like the Emsworths, either father or son. More to the point, he despised them. The old man came home a hero from the Second World War. Led some sort of escape from a Nazi prisoner of war camp. There was even a statue of him, holding an Enfield rifle and striking a fearless pose, in front of the Chambury library.

A hero he might have been; a lord he was not – despite demanding to be addressed as "Lord Emsworth." Shortly after the war, Reginald Emsworth had used his new found fame to develop a network of rich and powerful businessmen and politicians. Using those contacts, and with borrowed money, he had become wealthy. He used part of that wealth to *purchase* a Lordship. The man then sold his house in Chambury, a house that he claimed was later purchased by Rebecca Fleming, and had bought an imposing estate some ten miles from the village. Now, for reasons Dylan simply could not comprehend, the man wanted his old house back. Why, thought Dylan, does the old fool want to die in a modest house when he could, just as easily and far more comfortably, depart this world in a mansion?

Could it be, Dylan wondered, that Lord Emsworth has money problems? For a mansion the size of his, the man seemed to have very few servants or staff – just his unbearable butler, two gardeners, and a small kitchen staff. And there were rumors of extravagant spending by his third wife and his son.

Dylan hoped and prayed that his involvement with the Emsworth's would be concluded just as soon as possible. In the meantime, he was determined to squeeze every quid he could out of his unwelcome entanglement with "Lord" Emsworth.

#####

Back in Lord Emsworth's study, his son, Henry Emsworth, poured himself and his father a brandy. Henry handed one of the glasses to Lord Emsworth and then sat down on the chair opposite his father.

"Father, in case that idiot can't convince the Yank to sell the house, I'm sure I can."

"No, let Jones take care of this. I don't want you to get involved. And I don't want you seen anywhere near the Fleming house. If there's any pressure to be applied, we'll apply it to Jones. Damn, I never should have entrusted this matter to that simpleton."

Chapter 9

Chambury; Saturday, 17 April 2010: David Wallace placed a phone call to the offices of Dorrit and Dombey, the Cheltenham financial services firm that held his late aunt's funds. Even though it was Saturday, he held out some hope that there might be someone at the firm with whom he could talk.

The call was met with a voice recording, informing the caller that the firm was open from 9 a.m. to 4 p.m., every *weekday*. Unable to reach anyone at the firm, David decided to skim through the manuscript, *A Cotswold Diary*.

He finished reading the manuscript four hours later – the very first romance novel he had ever read. Catherine Cromwell, aka Rebecca Fleming, was quite the writer. No one, he was convinced, could ever imagine that an 84 year-old woman had penned the page-turner. David had, however, reached the end of an *unfinished* manuscript which left him wondering just how his aunt had intended to conclude the story. In fact, he discovered that he wanted very much to know how anyone could resolve the unfortunate and seemingly hopeless situation in which the spirited heroine of *A Cotswold Diary* had found herself in Chapter 36.

How hard, David asked himself, could it really be to write a romance novel? After all, all one had to do was type.

With Molly watching his every move, David inserted a sheet of paper between the paper table and the platen of his aunt's antique typewriter. He rotated the platen knobs until the top of the sheet of paper was visible and then moved the carriage to the right. So far, so good, he thought.

At the top of the sheet he typed: "Chapter 37." He then stared at the sheet for about ten minutes before attempting to type. An hour later he discovered that he had only typed a little more than one hundred words, and he wasn't at all pleased with the result. David removed the sheet he had been working on, crumpled it up, and tossed it into the wastebasket. Writing a romance novel, he decided while inserting a fresh sheet of paper, wasn't nearly as easy as he had imagined.

After five more false starts, and with an overflowing wastebasket, David came to the conclusion that – before attempting to write even one word more – he needed to think of the two main characters in the story as actual, living, breathing human beings rather than characters in a manuscript. That, he decided, required a walk. A nice long walk.

"Molly, how about the two of us taking another walk?"

Molly didn't have to be asked twice. She managed to race downstairs, retrieve her leash and walking collar, and then scurry back upstairs in a matter of seconds.

#####

As David was about to open the front gate, so as to begin the walk into the village, he noticed a pool of what appeared to be some sort of liquid under his Renault Twingo. Examining it closer he realized that it was radiator fluid. Opening the bonnet, his worst fears were realized: a seam at the top of the radiator had burst. While the car had, albeit just barely, got him to Chambury, it was clear that it was not going to go anywhere else – or at least not very far – until the radiator was resealed. That, he realized, would be like throwing good money after bad. The car, he was convinced, needed to "be put down." Besides that, he doubted that he had nearly enough money left to pay anyone to do all the repairs necessary to restore the old heap to running order – at least that required to pass the yearly MOT test.

It was then that David recalled that Dylan Jones had told him that "the everything" he had inherited included his aunt's car. That car, he thought, just might be kept in what he had previously thought to be an oversized garden shed located to the rear of the house.

David, with Molly at his heels, opened the door of the shed to find what appeared to be a shiny new Vauxhall Astra. Examining it closer, he decided that it was more likely a four-year old Astra, but in near showroom condition. He then took note of a gate, wide enough to allow a car to pass through, located on the west side of the stacked stone wall that surrounded the front and sides of his aunt's house.

David opened the driver's side door and was about to take a seat in the car when Molly beat him to it. The dog pushed past him, leapt into the car, and took a position on the passenger side.

"So, Molly, I take it that you like to ride in cars.

That sounds like a nice idea, but we need a car key first."

Molly, for the first time since David had met her, let out a low "woof" and placed her snout against the car's glove compartment. David opened the glove box and, sure enough, found the key to the ignition. There was also a remote control device in the glove box. That, he assumed, would be the remote necessary to open the side gate.

"Molly, sometimes you are scary smart. Well, now that we've got the key and gate opener, I suppose we should take the car for a spin."

#####

Two hours later David and Molly returned to the Fleming house. It took two trips to unload the purchases of the day: groceries for David and a cuddly toy teddy bear for Molly.

That evening David placed the cuddly toy in Molly's crate. "All right, Molly, time for bed. Tonight you'll sleep in your crate and I'll sleep in my bed."

The dog whimpered softly but, with some encouragement, entered the crate. David then closed and locked the crate's door.

David lay in bed for several hours, unable to sleep. He wanted a drink, and wanted it badly. Rising from the bed, he walked downstairs and opened the door to Molly's crate. Taking the cuddly toy in hand, he led the dog back to the bedroom.

David, with Molly lying next to him, went to sleep.

Chapter 10

Chambury; Sunday, 18 April 2010: About an hour before sunrise, David woke with a start. He pulled off his bedcovers and raced to his aunt's office. After a brief stretching session, Molly followed.

David inserted a clean sheet of paper in the typewriter. He then began to type. He did not stop until 4 p.m. that afternoon. Molly was left to her own devices. She chose, for the most part, to remain in the office.

The conclusion to *A Cotswold Diary* had come to David as if in a dream. In that dream he had viewed – as if sitting in a movie theatre – what now made up the final chapters of *A Cotswold Diary*. All that had been left for him to do was type, as fast as he could, what he had seen and heard in that dream.

"Molly, how about a walk?" said David once he had typed the very last word of *A Cotswold Diary*.

Once the walk had been completed, David returned to the office and proceeded to read, from start to finish, the now completed manuscript. That evening, shortly before bedtime, he placed the completed manuscript into a large manila envelope and addressed it to the Passionate Word Literary Agency, in care of Mildred Pankhurst.

Some fifty miles away, in her Cheltenham flat, Mildred Pankhurst sealed and stamped her letter to

Catherine Cromwell. That letter, she was confident, would finally lead to a face-to-face meeting with Catherine.

#####

Detective Constable Tommi Blake loved Sundays. It was one of her days off and allowed her to spend the entire day – assuming there were no requests for her presence at HQ – with Joyce, her younger sister. Just looking at the two women, one would never guess they were related, much less sisters. Auburn-haired Tommi was tall, athletic, and serious. Joyce, a lively blonde, was a full six inches shorter and an ebullient extrovert. Both women were pretty, but the more vibrant and outgoing Joyce had always been the one that attracted the boys.

The two women had lived in the same house – a detached 1960's style two-story – their entire lives, although Tommi was seriously considering moving to her very own flat. Their parents had moved to New Zealand a few months earlier, their father having accepted a temporary position at the University of Auckland.

Tommi had decided on a career in law enforcement at age 13; Joyce was still trying to decide her future. For the time being, however, she was satisfied with her position at the Chambury library. Over dinner that evening, discussion had turned to their respective bosses.

"Miss Kowalski has been brooding more than usual," said Joyce, "and that's saying something. She seems terribly worried about something – her mood changed right after Wednesday night's council meeting. She won't tell me what they said that might have upset her so, but she's definitely worried."

"Joyce, Liliana Kowalski is *always* worried about something. She worries about people with dirty fingers turning the pages of 'her' books. She worries about kids using the library computers to surf for porn. She even worries about those people who fill in the crossword puzzles in the library's newspaper collection. And I'll never forget what that woman did to me when she thought I had torn a few pages out of one of her precious library magazines. Good grief, she had me thrown off the school lacrosse team – for an entire year!"

"She does have a tendency to overreact," said Joyce.

"Those were exactly my thoughts yesterday. She popped into the station and asked to see me. She handed me a plastic bag. Inside it was a sugar bowl, a bowl belonging to Rebecca Fleming's tea set. According to Liliana there was some residue at the bottom of the bowl. She asked that I have the residue tested – and to also check the bowl for fingerprints. She seems to think that someone was trying to poison Miss Fleming."

"But I thought that Miss Fleming drowned," said Joyce.

"That was the coroner's report, and I trust their work. Rebecca Fleming had water in her lungs when her body was found. She definitely drowned."

"So, what are you going to do with the sugar bowl?"

"I decided to play it safe and have it tested. We should have the results either tomorrow or Tuesday. My guess, though, is that Miss Fleming simply failed to keep a clean sugar bowl."

"True, but enough about my boss; you haven't said much about the new DCI. What's he like?"

"In a word, 'inscrutable.' Sometimes I think he detests the idea of being partnered with a female; other times I think he just doesn't care, one way or the other. The man, for some reason or another, wants me to wear my uniform – and this after I worked so hard to become a detective. And those damn glasses of his! I told you that he sometimes puts on tinted glasses. He says it somehow makes his job easier. I'm beginning to wonder about that.

"Then there's his reaction to the district. He didn't say as much but, on our drive around the area, I had the distinct impression that the man thinks we're just a bunch of dumb farmers. Do you know what he did when we happened to drive pass Alfie Clarkson, who happened to be taking a piss by the side of the road? DCI Grahame actually wanted to have him arrested for indecent exposure! I had to explain that old Alfie was at least a mile from the nearest loo and the poor man's most likely got a bladder the size of a peanut.

"I suppose that there's just not enough violent crime here to satisfy someone who has spent their entire career in London."

"Have you found out why he was transferred here?" asked Joyce.

"No, there's just a lot of rumors. No one seems to be even sure of exactly *how* he was transferred – a transfer from London to a station in Gloucestershire is almost unheard of. I did find out, however, that the man's wife was killed by a hit-and-run driver just a year ago. They haven't as yet caught whoever did it."

Joyce shook her head. "That's horrible, and probably explains why the man is so, as you said, 'inscrutable.'"

"I suppose so but, speaking of 'accidents,' how are the village's plans for Lord Emsworth's 90th birthday going? Is Miles Shrewsbury still intent on staging a re-enactment of Emsworth's escape from the Germans?"

"The plans, I'm happy to say, are now fixed – and Mr. Shrewsbury's proposal was voted down. The *Parents Against Firearms* group went absolutely bonkers when they heard about his proposal. It's been decided to simply have an orderly march down the high street to be followed by a ceremony on the square. The village has purchased ten copies of Lord Emsworth's autobiography and he has agreed to autograph them. Miss Kowalski has consented to hand them out to ten of our top-performing village school children. Everyone is looking forward to the ceremonies."

"Yeah," said Tommi, wincing.

Chapter 11

Chambury; Monday, 19 April 2010: When Monday morning arrived, David decided to forego a walk into town. Instead, he was determined to meet with his late aunt's financial advisor. Shortly after eight, he, with Molly perched contentedly in the Astra's passenger seat, commenced the drive to Cheltenham.

At a brief stop on the way he posted the manila envelope containing the now completed manuscript of *A Cotswold Diary.* He held out little hope, however, that Mildred Pankhurst of the Passionate Word Literary Agency would find his effort acceptable. He did wonder, however, what comments she might provide. In fact, he realized, he very much wanted to receive her feedback.

The offices of Dorrit and Dombey were located in an impressive stone building a few blocks west of Cheltenham's Art Gallery and Museum. Five doors down, David noticed, were the offices of the Passionate Word Literary Agency – albeit in a much less impressive edifice.

After a brief wait, David was ushered into the large and imposing office of Andrew Dombey. Dombey appeared to be a man in his late fifties. He was of average height but had the build – and handshake – of an athlete. Based on the photos on the wall behind the man's desk, it was clear that he had indeed been an athlete – a cricket player for the venerable Cheltenham Cricket Club.

"Sir," said David, attempting to get right to the point, "I'm the sole heir to my late aunt's estate, the estate of Rebecca Fleming. I've …'

Before David could finish his well rehearsed introductory remarks, Dombey, his face gone pale, interrupted. "Miss Fleming has died? No one informed me of that. My God, I can't believe it. She was so full of life the last time she visited."

"She passed away nearly a month ago; I had assumed you were aware of that."

"No, I was not. Can't hardly believe it. I realize that she was well up in terms of years but I must say I was convinced that she would live to 100, if not beyond. Mr. Wallace, that dear woman was my client for more than twenty-five years. I formed quite a liking for your aunt; she was a remarkable woman and had quite the head for stock picking. My condolences."

"Thank you," David replied, although he felt guilty for accepting condolences for the death of a woman he barely remembered.

"Mr. Wallace, what can I do for you?" asked Dombey.

"I have a problem, actually several problems," said David. "I'd very much appreciate your help."

David attempted to summarize his situation. He explained that he was nearly destitute and needed money so as to unencumber his inheritance and that he hoped to use the funds being held by Dorrit and Dombey in his aunt's account to achieve that end.

Dombey raised his hand. "Mr. Wallace, would you

please repeat what you recall this Dylan Jones chap told you. Particularly about what he claimed is needed to free up your inheritance."

Once David had completed a recitation of his conversation with Dylan, Dombey said: "I would like to tell you something in confidence. May I trust you to not repeat this?"

"Certainly," David replied.

"Your aunt mentioned something about this chap before; as I recall it was about two or three months ago. I had a member of my staff check up on him. All that I can tell you now is that he is, in my personal opinion, a rather dodgy character. Furthermore, there is no need to borrow any funds whatsoever to unencumber your inheritance. The monies in Rebecca's account at Dorrit and Dombey are simply part of her estate. As such, they are yours, subject to the inheritance tax. Those funds, however, should be more than sufficient – even after taxes – to pay the entire tax and, as well, leave you with what I would estimate to be about a quarter million pounds."

David was stunned. "A quarter million pounds! That's fantastic. What a relief."

"Mr. Wallace, have this Jones person meet with us tomorrow morning at 9 a.m. sharp. Accept no excuses. Tell him to bring the will, death certificate, and all the relevant paperwork with him. This entire matter can be resolved in a matter of minutes – without any need for you to become further involved with Dylan Jones. And, Mr. Wallace, let me remind you that everything that has been discussed in this office today is to be kept absolutely confidential."

David nodded his head and, sensing the meeting

was over, rose from his chair. Andrew Dombey, however, was not finished.

"Mr. Wallace, one more matter before you go." With that Dombey reached into his desk and retrieved a stack of pound notes. "Consider this a loan. There should be 500 pounds there; that should keep you until this matter is concluded. If not, let me know if you need more."

"Thank you, sir. I'm sure that will do for now. Thank you so much for your time and the loan."

The meeting concluded, Dombey walked David to the door of his office. "Is that Molly I see?" said Dombey as he opened the door to the reception area. Molly, who had been lying on the floor next to the receptionist's desk, leapt to her feet and raced to David's side.

"Yes, sir," David replied.

"Well, young man, take good care of her. Miss Rebecca doted on that animal."

David unlocked the driver's side door of the Astra and immediately stood to one side. By now he had learned that Molly was keen on being the first one in the car.

"Ladies first," said David as Molly made herself comfortable.

Checking his mobile phone, David saw that Dylan Jones had left three voicemail messages. David placed a return call to Jones.

Dylan Jones agreed, after a somewhat uncomfortable pause in the conversation, to the meeting at Dorrit and Dombey. He then assured David that he had a serious buyer for the Fleming house, and that the two of them could discuss that matter once the meeting with Andrew Dombey was concluded.

Once the call was finished, David turned the key in the ignition and headed back to Chambury. Rather than driving directly back to the Fleming house, however, he intended to make one brief stop … at the Chambury library.

Chapter 12

Chambury; Monday, 19 April 2010: Liliana Kowalski, sitting behind her immaculately arranged desk in the Chambury library, was deep in thought. She was thinking, as usual, about books. To say that Liliana liked books would be a colossal understatement; she absolutely and passionately adored books. She particularly loved the smell of books – especially old, expensively bound books. Her cloistered life revolved around books and bookshelves; she could even recite – from memory – the classes, divisions, and sections of her beloved Dewey Decimal System.

For more than twenty years Liliana had also loved her job at the Chambury library. It had been her home away from home. She realized, however, that changes – radical changes – were imminent. She also concluded that she was powerless to stop those changes. Any hope for an escape from the impending disaster facing her and her beloved books had evaporated with the reading of Rebecca Fleming's last will and testament.

Liliana's thoughts were disturbed by the sound of the opening and closing of the door to the library. A man … and a dog … stood by the door. Not just any man or any dog; it was David Wallace and Molly. He was saying something to Liliana's assistant, the young and pretty Miss Joyce Blake. Joyce, Liliana noted with disapproval, was giggling.

Joyce, face aglow, rose from her desk and walked hurriedly to Liliana's workstation. "Miss Kowalski, this gentlemen wants to know if he can bring his dog into the library. It does seem to be a very well behaved animal. In fact, I do believe that it's Molly, Miss Fleming's dog. What should I tell him?"

"You know quite well that dogs are not allowed," said Liliana."

"Yes, ma'am, I'll let him know," said Joyce as she was about to walk away.

"Wait," said Liliana. "Tell him that I'll make an exception this one time. Just bring the dog back to my workstation and out of sight of any library patrons. As for you, Miss Blake, do stop flirting with that man."

#####

Guyton-upon-Cham; Monday, 19 April 2010: DC Tommi Blake answered the phone. She listened for about three minutes before thanking the caller and returning the phone to its base. The lab results on Rebecca Fleming's sugar bowl had been a surprise. What was even more surprising, however, was DCI Grahame's reaction.

Tommi was of the opinion that Inspector Grahame was either incredibly stupid or else his brilliance and insight were beyond the capability of ordinary mortal human beings to comprehend. She was definitely leaning, however, toward incredibly stupid.

#####

Chambury; Monday, 19 April 2010: Liliana, with Molly now lying on the floor beside her desk, watched David Wallace with growing interest. The man had a large manila envelope in hand and walked, without hesitation, to one of the library's two computer consoles. Seeing her, he nodded his head and whispered "Thank you."

The two computer screens had been placed so that Liliana could see whatever their users happened to be viewing. She had directed their placement in order to stop anyone from surfing the web for anything Liliana might consider "inappropriate." Any teenage boy who happened to view swimsuit models, for example, would find himself banned from the library.

Liliana watched, with increasing attentiveness, as David Wallace opened the large envelope and removed a number of newspaper clippings. She could see, from the computer screen, that he was viewing a Polish-to-English translation program.

Unable to contain her curiosity, Liliana took a seat next to David. "Mr. Wallace, I see that you seem to be translating something from Polish to English. I read, write, and speak Polish fluently. I'm quite sure that I can provide you with a translation much faster, and far more accurately, than any computer software program. If you like, I'd be happy to translate these for you."

David, realizing that it would likely take hours to translate, word-by-word, the articles via the computer, readily accepted Liliana's offer. He followed her to a large, enclosed room at the very back of the library. The walls of the room were lined with bookshelves and most of those shelves were filled with expensively bound books. The room also contained a large wooden table and four chairs. There was a book, lying open, on the table – along with several small jars containing a clear liquid and a dizzying array of other items, including spools of thread, several odd-looking needles, a roll of binding tape, and what appeared to be a block of beeswax.

"Have a seat, Mr. Wallace, while I move these items out of the way so as to give us more room." Then, pointing to the open book, she added: "This happens to be a first edition of Mark Twain's *Innocents Abroad*. I'm afraid someone did not give it the care it deserves. When it comes to books, some people can be complete and utter philistines."

"So," said David, "this is where you repair the library's books. I suppose that keeps you busy."

"Most of the books in this room," said Liliana, pointing to the shelves, "are actually mine. Any of the library's books that need repair are worked on during the day. I work on my own collection in the evenings. And, rather than repair, most of my work is dedicated to restoration. But, enough of that, let's take a closer look at your news clippings."

David spread the newspaper clippings on the table's surface.

"Ah," said Liliana, "these are all clippings from Polish newspapers. No, wait a minute, several are from British papers. I suppose you've already read those, of course."

"Yes, they seem to be articles about certain members of a World War II British Army platoon. They're referred to in several of the articles as the 'Lost Platoon' and a few clippings even include photos and names of some of the platoon members. From what I've read, most of the members of the platoon were either killed or captured by the

Germans. Those that were captured were sent to a prisoner of war camp in Germany. Then there's something about a 'death march;' not sure what that's all about though."

"Evidently they don't teach you Yanks about the death marches the Nazis conducted during the last months of the war. The Nazis didn't want their prisoners of war or their concentration camp inmates to fall into the hands of the Allied forces. They didn't want to leave any witnesses to their atrocities so they either killed the poor souls outright or marched them away from the advancing Allied forces. The concentration camp inmates were in truly terrible shape and the POWs weren't much better off. They were forced to march through one of the worst winters in history."

"Why do you think my aunt would be collecting these clippings?"

"Your aunt? These are Rebecca's? Where on earth did you find them?"

"I found them ... actually Molly found them ... in the mud room in the rear of the house. They were on the same shelf that's used to store Molly's collar and leash."

"That's quite strange. Rebecca never once mentioned that she had any interest in the 'Lost Platoon.' The story of its only survivor, however, is quite well known in the village. Did you notice the statue in front of the library, the nine-foot tall soldier holding a rifle?"

"Yes," said David. "But I've got to admit that I didn't take the time to read the plaque on the monument."

"The statue is in honor of Lord Reginald Emsworth, the only member of the 'Lost Platoon' to survive the war. He, in fact, is still with us. According to the story, Emsworth managed to take a rifle away from one of the Nazi guards. He then shot and killed several other guards. Emsworth and three other prisoners were able to escape and, for a brief period, elude the Nazis.

"The little group attempted to make their way to the Allied lines but had to fight their way through retreating Nazi troops. Only Emsworth survived to tell the tale. The man shot and killed at least two dozen Nazis, and then killed three more with his bare hands after running out of ammunition. Sadly, he was the only one to make it to safety."

"Ah," said David, "quite an impressive accomplishment. You said he's still alive. Does he live in the village?"

"He used to live in the village, but he now resides in an impressive manor house about ten miles to the west. The man still leads, from what I'm told, a quite active life although he'll be ninety soon. In fact, a ceremony is to be held in the village next month to celebrate his birthday."

"So, again," asked David, "why do you think my aunt was collecting these newspaper clippings? Seems as if she could have just met with this Lord Emsworth if she was interested in his story."

"That I don't know," said Liliana, frowning. "Allow me to examine the clippings from the Polish newspapers. Perhaps that will provide an explanation. But, first of all, just what is that?" asked Liliana, picking up the Polish car hire receipt.

"It was in the envelope with the clippings," replied David. "I take it that aunt Rebecca made a trip to Poland several weeks ago."

"That's odd, she did take holiday recently, but she told me she was traveling to France. She said something about meeting an old school chum there. Not sure why she would have been in Poland. Nor why she never mentioned it."

David also wondered just why Liliana, supposedly his aunt's "dear friend," would have been unaware of the trip to Poland. Then again, he wondered just why Liliana Kowalski had pinched his aunt's sugar bowl.

Liliana thumbed through the Polish newspaper clippings, pausing for a minute or two upon reaching one article. At the top of the article were two photos, one of a young man in a rather unusual looking military uniform. The other was of a very old man, wearing the same military style cap as the young man featured in the first photo. Several of the words in the article had been underlined in red ink.

"Mr. Wallace, all of these clippings are also about the 'Lost Platoon' and the Nazi death marches. I'm guessing that Rebecca was simply researching those events. Perhaps she intended to write an article, or possibly even a book about those matters. I really need to get back to my post now, but if you'll leave the clippings with me I'll peruse them this afternoon and let you know if I find anything of interest. Do leave them with me and I'll return them, and their translations, to you at Rebecca's house this evening."

#####

Guyton-upon-Cham; Monday, 19 April 2010: DC Tommi Blake placed a call to the Chambury library. It was answered on its first ring by her sister, Joyce.

"Joyce," said Tommi, "is Liliana there?"

"Yes, she's here. She just finished some sort of meeting with the cute American I was telling you about. Just hold the phone and I'll get her."

As Tommi Blake waited for Liliana to come to the phone, she simply could not believe what she had been ordered, by DCI Grahame, to tell the woman.

#####

Chambury; Monday, 19 April 2010: David took a seat on the oversize armchair in the drawing room. While it was late April, the evening was quite chilly and the fire in the fireplace provided the room with a warm, comfortable, and almost homey feeling.

Molly evidently thought that there was room enough for two and joined David on the chair. Together, the twosome watched the dancing flames. While it is impossible to know just what Molly might have been thinking, David was reflecting on the past several days – a period in which his life seemed to have made another astonishing turnaround. This time, however, things appeared to have changed for the better.

It was, however, nearly 11 p.m. and Liliana Kowalski had yet to return the collection of clippings. Well, he thought, if the librarian was that keen on keeping some news clippings – and his aunt's sugar bowl – then so be it. He had better things to do, like claim his inheritance, sell this house and return to Texas.

But there was at least one nagging thought. If Liliana Kowalski and his late aunt had been such close friends, why hadn't his aunt sought her help in translating the clippings? Was his aunt able to read Polish? And why had she told Liliana that she was traveling to France when, instead, her destination had been Poland?

Chapter 13

Cheltenham; Tuesday, 20 April 2010: The meeting at the Cheltenham offices of Dorrit and Dombey was concluded shortly before noon. The four attendees were David Wallace, Dylan Jones, Andrew Dombey, and Edward Tulkinghorn, the latter a solicitor employed by the firm. While the solicitor noted that it would take a few days for all the paperwork to be finalized, he assured David that he was now the legal owner of his late aunt's estate.

Once the solicitor and Dylan Jones had left, Dombey explained to David that his late aunt's account with the firm of Dorrit and Dombey was now in his name. After payment of the inheritance taxes and other fees, Dombey estimated that the balance remaining in the account would be on the order of 240,000 pounds. He left it to David to decide whether those funds should be left in that account or transferred to a bank of David's choice.

David agreed to leave the funds with Dorrit and Dombey – as well as to establish a checking account in his own name with the firm's bank – at least until he sold his late aunt's house and returned to the States. After thanking Andrew Dombey for his help, David – and Molly – exited the offices of Dorrit and Dombey. There, standing on the pavement directly in front of the offices, was Dylan Jones.

Dylan asked David to join him for lunch at a pub a few doors down from Dorrit and Dombey. David agreed, but only after telling Dylan that he was not yet prepared to place his aunt's house – now his house – up for sale.

"I need," David explained, "some time to think about this. I want to determine, for example, just what to do with Molly. I'm torn between leaving her here or taking her to the States with me."

The more David attempted to justify his hesitation in selling the house, the more he began to wonder just what was *really* holding him back. After all, as Dylan Jones had explained, there was an buyer eager to purchase the house and to pay a price well above its market value.

David, however, completely "lost the plot" when an extremely attractive brunette entered the pub.

#####

Mildred Pankhurst placed her usual order at the bar of the Pickled Pig pub, paid for the food and drink, and then found an empty table. There were, she observed, two rather attractive men on the other side of the room. Both, she noted, had been staring at her.

One of the men, she noticed, had a dog with him, a yellow Lab. The dog was sitting on its haunches next to the man, its head lying on the man's knee. The man's hand was resting on the dog's head. Mildred thought that, should she ever meet that man – and his dog – she would like them both.

#####

Edward Tulkinghorn tapped on the door of Andrew Dombey's office. "Come in, Edward," said Dombey.

"Andy, the more I think about this morning's

meeting, the more I believe we should contact the police."

"What on earth for?" asked Dombey. "It was just a simple transfer of an estate. Why would you want to contact the police?"

"Rebecca Fleming died under what I would consider unusual circumstances. You said yourself that you were told that she was found facedown in a pond. Then this American, who admits he barely knew Miss Fleming, suddenly shows up in England – as sole heir to Miss Fleming's estate. I recommend that, to protect the reputation of Dorrit and Dombey, we inform the police in Guyton of the American's inheritance."

"I really don't think it's necessary but, if you're truly worried about it, then please do contact the police. Just make sure to tell them that we're doing this out of an abundance of caution."

Edward Tulkinghorn placed a call to the Guyton-upon-Cham police station. His call was directed to a DCI Grahame.

"Detective Chief Inspector Grahame here; what can I do for you?"

#####

Chambury; Tuesday, 20 April 2010: David and Molly returned to Chambury at around 3 p.m. David decided to park the Astra on a street behind the library rather than proceed directly home. He intended to ask Liliana about the newspaper clippings as well as request their return.

David opened the door to the library to find it empty with the exception of a nearly frantic Joyce Blake. The young woman was holding a "CLOSED" sign in her hand.

"I'm terribly sorry, Mr. Wallace, but the library's closed. I'm just about to place a sign on the door and lock up. You'll have to come back tomorrow."

"I'd just like to talk with Miss Kowalski," said David. "Is she here?"

"You haven't heard?" asked Joyce. "Mr. Wallace, the police are looking for Miss Kowalski. In fact, a few minutes after her meeting with you yesterday, she received a phone call and then left the library without saying a word. No one has seen her since. The police are, I believe, now searching her flat."

"Searching her flat? What on earth for?"

"I'm really not supposed to say. But, according to my sister – Tommi is a member of the local police service – they seem to believe that Miss Kowalski may have poisoned your aunt. In fact, at this very moment I'm told that they are exhuming your aunt's body."

"My God," said David, "my God. I know Miss Kowalski is a bit on the grim side, but I would never had thought her capable of murder."

"Nor me. Mr. Wallace, once I got to know Miss Kowalski, I found her to be a good, decent person. Now, she may not have a sense of humor, and she may like books more than people, but she was not – and is not, in my opinion – someone who would harm a fellow human. In fact, she and your aunt were very close. Miss Kowalski had only good things to say about her."

"Then," asked David, "why did she suddenly disappear?"

David led Molly across and up the street. This entire

situation, he thought, is bizarre. First, from out of the blue he discovers that he is the sole heir of his aunt's estate – the estate of a woman who he can barely remember. Now he is informed that the poor woman may have been poisoned. Just thinking about it gave him a headache.

Stopping in front of the mailbox rental storefront, David tied Molly's leash around the pole in front of the shop and entered. The same man was there and just as unfriendly as ever.

David opened the mailbox to find a single letter, a letter from the Passionate Word Literary Agency. David left the shop, untied Molly's leash, and crossed the street to one of the two village pubs. The Bashful Badger, a pub as well as a four-guestroom B&B, was located directly across the pedestrian zone from his aunt's mailbox.

Resisting the temptation to order a beer, or to indulge in the pub's daily special: fish and chips with mushy peas, David instead ordered a lemonade and a bag of crisps and took a seat at an empty table. He then opened the letter. It was from Mildred Pankhurst.

> My dear Catherine, I am returning to you, by special delivery, the manuscript of your novel: *Obsession*. It will be arriving at your post box at approximately noon on Wednesday. Please pick it up as soon as possible as I have something of the utmost importance to

```
discuss with you.
```
Curious, thought David, before inserting the short note back into its envelope. He could only wonder what Mildred Pankhurst wanted to discuss and just why it was so urgent. The woman had also, he noted, failed to explain just where she and Catherine were to discuss those matters of "utmost importance." Those thoughts, however, quickly slipped from his mind and were replaced by the matter of Liliana Kowalski and the possible murder of his aunt..

Chapter 14

Lord Emsworth's Manor House, Chambury; Tuesday, 20 April 2010: Lord Emsworth's face was on the verge of turning crimson, the veins in the old man's forehead were protruding, and Dylan Jones had taken on the look of a man on his way to the gallows.

"Damn it, Jones, you told me the Yank would be ready to sell once the estate was settled. Well, damn it, the estate is now settled! Now you tell me he wants some more time to 'think things over.' Which is it man, is he going to sell, or spend the next few years thinking things over?"

Henry, Lord Emsworth's son, felt compelled to pile on. "Yes, Jones, what the hell happened? You told us that the Yank was a penniless drunk who would sell his mother to get back to the States. Now you're feeding us quite a different story. So, answer my father and be quick about it."

"As I told you both, the Fleming woman had funds I knew nothing about. The Yank now has the house, its furnishings, the car, *and* a bundle of cash. He's not nearly as desperate today as he was last week. In fact, I imagine he thinks he's sitting rather pretty."

At that moment Wooster, Lord Emsworth's butler, appeared at the door to the study. "Yes, Wooster, what is it?" asked Lord Emsworth impatiently.

"Your lordship, please excuse the interruption but I've just learned of some news in the village that may be of interest to you. Perhaps, in fact, it may be of interest to all three of you."

"Yes, go on, Wooster. What is this news that is so bloody important?"

"Sir, the police believe that Miss Rebecca Fleming may have been poisoned. I am told that they are exhuming the body at this very moment. Furthermore, the village's head librarian, a Miss Liliana Kowalski, is evidently the suspect in this dastardly deed. She, however, has evidently fled."

Wooster's remarks were met with stunned silence.

Lord Emsworth was the first to recover. "Thank you, Wooster. That will do. We'd like to be alone now."

Once Wooster had closed the door behind him, Lord Emsworth turned to Dylan Jones. "Jones, what do you know about this librarian?"

"Your lordship, I only know that Liliana Kowalski was supposedly Rebecca Fleming's closest friend. She was a frequent visitor at her home. Of course, she was also quite devastated when she learned that Miss Fleming's entire estate was going to the Yank."

"Devastated enough to have poisoned her friend?" asked Lord Emsworth.

"Liliana Kowalski is a very angry woman. I would not put anything past her," Dylan replied. "She did not, however, know that Rebecca Fleming left her out of the will until I informed her of it *after* the death of the Fleming woman. Furthermore, how could she have poisoned the Fleming woman when according to the police – and the original autopsy – Rebecca

Fleming *drowned?*"

"Damn it," said Lord Emsworth, "I don't care if she drowned, was poisoned, stabbed, speared, clubbed, shot, or drawn and quartered. I simply expect you to fulfill your promise. You do remember, don't you, that you promised me that the Yank would sell me the house?"

"Yes," Dylan replied. "I promised, and I assure you that he will sell. This matter about the poisoning, however, may complicate matters. It may take a little longer."

"Unacceptable! Jones, I'm sure that you can find a way to use the situation to speed the Yank's decision. Let him know that this rather messy matter can be quickly resolved by simply selling the house and returning to the States. Jones, one should never let a crisis go to waste."

Chapter 15

Chambury; Tuesday, 20 April 2010: David, with Molly resting beside him on the oversize chair in the drawing room, was deep in thought. He was upset with the idea that his late aunt was to undergo yet another autopsy. While he could barely remember the woman, it seemed awful that her body would be subjected to the indignity of yet further dissection – or whatever might be involved. Why, he wondered, couldn't she be left to rest in peace?

Then again, he realized, there was certainly something strange going on. Why had the police first claimed that his aunt had drowned and now suddenly suspect a poisoning? If she had been poisoned, why was she found lying face down in the pond behind the house? Then he realized that he had yet to venture beyond the rear garden, and had yet to even take a look at that pond.

David left Molly snoozing contentedly on "their" chair, exited the rear door of the house and walked through the back garden. There, he noted, a footpath that led through a group of Scot Pines which he assumed must lead to the pond. As he entered the cluster of trees he saw that there was a piece of fabric on a tree branch at about shoulder height. He removed the piece, noticing that it was a fragment of flannel material of a flowered pattern that included what appeared to be a portion of a hem. Placing the piece in his pocket, he continued his trek toward what he hoped would be a pond.

That walk required a fairly steep uphill climb. Upon arriving at its peak, David saw that he had reached his destination. The pond before him was no more than 50 meters long and perhaps 30 meters wide. It was shallow its entire length and width. David guessed that no where was it deeper than two or three meters, and far less than that on the edge he was facing.

On the far side of the pond lay a broad meadow, its fields abloom with wild flowers. Beyond that was a rustic one-story stone cottage. Other than for the cottage, David could see no other structures of any kind behind his aunt's house.

A number of questions raced through his mind. What would possess his aunt to walk to the pond? How could an elderly, sick woman manage such a trek? More so, how could an elderly, sick, *and poisoned* woman have done so?

#####

David Wallace didn't know it, but he was being watched. "Miles, look out the window," said Maggie Shrewsbury, one of the two (human) residents of the stone cottage. "There's someone nosing around the pond. I do believe it's that Yank."

Miles Shrewsbury raced to the window. "Yep, that's him. I saw him and Molly in the village Saturday morning. That's definitely the Yank."

"Well," said Maggie, "you know what they say: the criminal always returns to the scene of the crime."

"For God's sake, Maggie, you don't know if the

man's a criminal or not."

"They're all lunatics, those Americans, always shooting each other."

"You've got to stop believing everything you read in the *Guardian,*" said Miles, shaking his head in disgust.

"I'll stop reading the *Guardian* when you stop watching *Sky News*, old man!"

#####

David had avoided disturbing, or even entering his late aunt's bedroom until now. It was, after all, *her* room. He decided, however, to examine the room and its contents. While he had no idea as to what to look for, he felt that there was much more to the death of his aunt than he had been told.

Rebecca Fleming's bedroom was immaculate, as neat and orderly as the rest of the house. David searched the bureau drawers and the closet without finding anything out of the ordinary. He then examined the array of framed photographs aligned on top of the bureau. While most were of people he did not recognize, two were quite familiar. One was a photograph of a young woman and her six year old son – his mother and him some 26 years ago. The other was a photo of Dylan Jones. The inscription on that picture was: "Your friend in need, Dylan."

David wondered just what "Your friend in need" meant, and replaced the photograph on the bureau. He then got down on all fours and peered under the bed. The only thing there was what looked to be a large, rolled-up poster.

David unrolled what he had thought to be a poster to discover that it was actually an old map of a portion of Europe, principally the countries of France, Germany, Poland, Switzerland, and Hungary. Someone, possibly his aunt, had placed X's at various positions on the map. Beside each X was a date. The earliest was 18 December 1944 and the latest was 23 February 1945.

Several towns in Germany, as well as two towns in Poland, were also circled on the map. Those circled towns, along with the Polish newspaper clippings, gave more weight to David's conviction that there was something about Poland that was of more than casual interest to his aunt.

Finding nothing more of interest in the bedroom, David decided to walk upstairs and investigate the office. While he had spent hours in there, working on the manuscript of *A Cotswold Diary*, he hadn't thought of looking for anything that might explain his aunt's death or her interest in Poland.

David first decided to scan the bookshelves. Most of the books on one side of the room were about investing. The volumes on the other side were mostly romance novels, including the ones penned by Catherine Cromwell. Two of the books on a lower shelf, however, were devoted to learning the Polish language. One was a Polish to English dictionary and the other was a Berlitz guide to learning Polish. Both books seemed to have received considerable use. The remainder of the books on that shelf were volumes about the Second World War. One of those, David noted, was a book titled: *The Last Escape: The untold story of Allied prisoners of war in Europe 1944-1945,* by John Nichol.

David then examined the contents of his aunt's file

cabinets. Two contained nothing other than office supplies – typewriter ribbons, correction fluid, notepads, and a large number of reams of paper. The third cabinet consisted of hanging files, all but one of which contained draft copies of the romance novels written by his aunt, under the pen name of Catherine Cromwell. One of the hanging files was, however, empty. It was labeled with the word, *Obsession.*

Chapter 16

Chambury; Tuesday, 20 April 2010: Mildred Pankhurst arrived at the village of Chambury shortly after 9 p.m. She parked her car in a pay and display lot and, after retrieving her overnight bag from the boot, walked into the village proper. The Bashful Badger pub was, as she had discovered on the Google map of the village, located almost directly across from the mailbox rental shop.

Mildred's room was, as she had insisted when reserving it, situated directly above the pub's bar, as well as being on the pedestrian zone side. The owner had warned her that the two rooms in the rear would be far quieter but she had insisted on the room facing the street. Once in that room, Mildred drew the curtains aside. From that vantage point she had a clear view of the mailbox rental shop.

Confident that her plans for tomorrow would go well, Mildred decided to walk downstairs and order a sandwich and glass of white wine. After ordering, Mildred took a seat at the only empty table left in the pub.

"Ah," said a man as he approached the same table, "Given up on the Pickled Pig, I see. Mind if I join you?"

Mildred thought the man looked familiar but could not place him. "Not at all," she replied as the man took the seat directly opposite her.

"My name is Dylan Jones. I believe I saw you earlier today in Cheltenham."

It was then that Mildred remembered. Dylan Jones, she realized, was one of the two men that she had noticed were staring at her when she had taken lunch in Cheltenham earlier that day. There was no way, however, that she intended to admit she remembered him.

"I'm terribly sorry," said Mildred, "but I'm afraid you have the advantage. Have we met?"

"No," replied Dylan, his face showing disappointment. "I just happened to be in the Pickled Pig pub when you walked in. I was sitting with another chap and couldn't help but notice you. I do hope I'm not being too bold."

"Not as long as you stay on that side of the table," said Mildred.

Dylan wasn't quite sure if the attractive young woman was joking or not. Undeterred, he fell back on a tried and true approach, one the English have honed to perfection over the centuries.

"Lovely weather we're having, don't you think?"

"Yes," Mildred replied, "spring is certainly here. My name, by the way is Mildred, Mildred Pankhurst."

Dylan was quite sure that such an old-fashioned name simply did not fit the woman seated across from him but decided not to express that thought. "Do you live in Cheltenham?"

"Yes, I work for a small literary agency there."

"What brings you to our little village?"

"Oh, I just decided to take a day or two off from work. Tomorrow is supposed to be absolutely brilliant. The weather is simply too lovely to be cooped up inside on a day like that. And just what do you do, Mr. Jones?"

"I'm a financial advisor; my work is mostly into estates, wills, trusts, and that sort of thing. Not nearly so interesting, I would imagine, as working at a literary agency."

"Well," said Mildred, "I do love my job, although it can be rather frustrating sometimes."

"Frustrating?"

"Definitely. My most promising young author refuses to talk with me on the phone, to communicate by email, or even meet with me."

"That does sound frustrating," said Dylan, "but then I've heard that authors are an odd lot. Of course I would think they'd have to be to live out their lives sitting in front of a word processor and writing about the exciting lives they'll never experience – they're all living in cloud cuckoo land if you ask me."

Dylan's unflattering assessment of writers touched a nerve but Mildred restrained herself. "Perhaps, but just think how much poorer we'd all be without the likes of Shakespeare, Tolstoy, Twain, Eliot, Lewis, Dickens, or Austen."

"Ah, and just how long has it been since you've worked with a modern-day Shakespeare?"

Mildred was angry and embarrassed at the same time. "My authors may not be Shakespeares but thousands of women find them entertaining."

"Women?" asked Dylan, his eyebrows arched.

"I'm an agent for authors of romance novels and, before you say anything, let me tell you that it takes a certain gift to write a romance novel – and an even greater gift to write a truly outstanding romance novel."

"I'm quite sure," replied Dylan. Realizing that he was treading on dangerous ground, he decided to change the subject. "How long did you say that you'll be staying in our fair village?"

"I'll probably be leaving tomorrow. Now, if you'll excuse me, it's been a long day; I'm going to my room. Nice to have met you, Mr. Jones."

"My pleasure, Miss Pankhurst. Do have a good night."

#####

Dylan Jones sat at the table, watching the departure of Mildred Pankhurst. Things had, thought Dylan, not gone well. Not well at all. Should he be fortunate enough to meet the lovely Miss Pankhurst again, he vowed to be much more careful – and far more charming.

#####

Mogilany, Poland; Tuesday, 20 April 2010: Liliana had only traveled to Poland twice before. Those trips had been taken to bury the ashes of her parents, first her father and then her mother. Their request to spend eternity under the soil of a land in which they had experienced so much suffering and trauma had always baffled Liliana, but she had complied with their wishes.

Liliana's parents rarely talked about Poland, and when they did it was always with a look of sadness, if not despair, on their faces. Liliana did, however, learn to speak Polish – albeit with an English accent. That ability had now enabled her to find the same man who had been Rebecca Fleming's driver a few weeks earlier. The man recalled driving Rebecca to Mogilany, a small village some 15 kilometers south of Krakow, the very same village that had been cited in at least two of the Polish newspaper clippings.

After pointing out a small house near the village center, Liliana's driver dropped her off at a B&B, not far from the village's market square, where she had reserved a room. Its owner seemed somewhat uneasy when he noticed that she had no baggage with her, only a purse. She attempted to ease his concern by explaining that her luggage had been misplaced by the airline.

Liliana lay in bed that night trying to decide just what to do next. This was, after all, her very first experience as a fugitive from justice.

Chapter 17

Chambury; Wednesday, 21 April 2010: The temperature was a balmy – for England – 20 degrees Celsius, or 68 degrees Fahrenheit, when David and Molly set off on their morning walk. The twosome reached the bakery at shortly after 9 a.m. After purchasing a coffee and cinnamon bun, David found a seat at one of the bakery's outdoor tables. A few minutes later an attractive young woman took a seat at another table. David was quite positive that she was the same woman he had seen in the Pickled Pig pub in Cheltenham.

As Mildred Pankhurst took her first sip of coffee she noticed the man and dog seated at another table. There was something quite familiar about him, but she couldn't recall why she would think so. Suddenly the man looked up and their eyes met.

David Wallace had heard of "the thunderbolt," the sensation that the Italians call "colpo di fulmine," but had never, until that moment, experienced it. According to the Italians, once the thunderbolt hits you, your life is irrevocably changed. Nothing from thereon will ever be the same. David was, he feared, suddenly head over heels in love with a woman he didn't know, a woman who was now daintily munching on what appeared to be a raisin scone, and who – he was shocked to discover – was now actually talking to him.

"Lovely dog," said Mildred, "he has such beautiful eyes."

"It's a she;" David replied, his heart skipping beats, "her name is Molly. I've only had her for a few days but I've got to say that she has become my best friend."

Mildred smiled in response and then, quite suddenly, she remembered where she had seen the man before. He, like the man she had met the previous evening, had been staring at her when she was taking lunch at the Pickled Pig. But, before she could say anything, the man abruptly rose from his table, nodded to her, and then – with the dog at his heels – walked away.

Well, thought Mildred, it would appear that she hadn't made much of an impression on the man. Somehow she very much regretted that. But she realized that she needed to focus her attention on the matter at hand. That, she hoped, would be resolved sometime around noon.

David and Molly left the house, once again, at noon. He was curious to determine just what the package Mildred Pankhurst had sent – to Catherine Cromwell – might contain that could be of "the utmost importance." He was having a difficult time, however, attempting to clear his mind of the attractive woman he had so briefly talked to at the bakery that morning.

Part of him actually hoped that he would never see her again. What could he, a man accused of being at fault in a horrendous industrial accident; someone who, until a few days ago, had been a drunken fool, hope to offer any woman? Particularly *that* woman.

David walked directly to the mailbox rental store. As usual, the grim-faced man behind the counter turned his back on him. David decided to do something about that.

"Good afternoon," said David. "Lovely day, isn't it?"

The man behind the counter grunted.

David discovered that the only item in the mailbox was a large, thick envelope marked Express. It was not, however, the style of envelope he had expected. Rather than a plain beige package, this envelope was covered with a red-and-white checkerboard pattern.

David decided to walk across the street to the Bashful Badger, take a seat at an outside table, and open the package. About halfway across the street he noticed that Dylan Jones was seated at an outdoor table. Next to him was the strikingly beautiful woman he had so briefly conversed with that morning – the "Thunderbolt" woman.

Both Dylan and the woman were looking at him. For a brief moment he thought of turning around. He had, however, reached a point-of-no-return.

"Good afternoon, Mr. Wallace," said Dylan.

"Good afternoon to you, Mr. Jones."

David then nodded to the woman. She, however, seemed to be staring, not at him, but at his brightly patterned package.

David decided to not stop at the pub and, instead, headed directly for home.

Dylan Jones noticed that Mildred Pankhurst was staring at David Wallace, even as the man hurried away. He wasn't happy about that.

"Excuse me, Mr. Jones, I must be off. Nice chatting with you," said Mildred.

Mildred tried not to walk overly fast as she proceeded to follow the man with the brightly patterned package. It was bad enough, she thought, that the exceedingly talkative Dylan Jones had taken a seat next to her. Now she found herself following a man rather than the elusive Catherine Cromwell. Had a woman picked up the package, Mildred would have immediately confronted her. Now, however, she was at a loss as to just how to proceed. So, like a character in a spy movie, she found herself following a man and a dog to heaven knows where.

What, thought Mildred Pankhurst, do I do now?

Mildred, attempting to be as discreet as possible, followed the man and his dog for several blocks. She hung back as the man opened the gate to a lovely Victorian two-story. He then unlocked the front door and entered and closed it. The dog, it seemed, had chosen to remain outside.

Mildred gathered her courage and walked past the house, then continued on down the street until she came to a wooden bench where she took a seat. My entire plan, she thought, is falling apart.

After a few minutes, Mildred decided to retrace her steps. She still wasn't sure as to what to do next, but she was determined to not let this opportunity slip away.

As Mildred approached the house that the man – and her package – had entered, she noticed that the dog – her name, Mildred recalled, was Molly – had poked her head through the opening in the top of the gate. Mildred stopped, petted Molly, and then decided on a plan – well, sort of a plan.

Mildred opened the gate and walked to the front door of the house. Once there she drew a deep breath and knocked on the door.

A very surprised David Wallace opened the door.

"Hello again. We chatted at the bakery this morning. My name is Mildred Pankhurst and I was just walking by when I noticed that your dog seemed to be in distress." Mildred waited for a response but the man simply stood in the doorway, as if he were frozen to the spot.

"The poor thing had a thorn in her paw, the right front paw. I can't stand to see an animal in pain so I immediately removed the thorn. I hope you don't mind; I simply felt that I had to help."

David, having recovered his composure somewhat, was finally able to reply. "I don't mind at all, and I thank you – and Molly, I'm sure, thanks you. My name, by the way, is David Wallace. I was in such a hurry this morning that I'm afraid I forgot my manners."

Mildred did her best to peer around David and into the house. From what she could see, the house was exceptionally neat and tidy and she could definitely sense a woman's influence on its decorations. "My," said Mildred, "you do have a lovely home – and so beautifully decorated. My compliments to your wife."

"Thank you, but I'm not married. I just recently moved here and everything is pretty much the way it was prior to my move."

Mildred assessed the situation. The man said he

was not married and there was certainly no wedding ring on his finger. He had said, in addition, that he had just moved into the house. This was curious. Where was Catherine Cornwall and why did the man pick up a package, addressed to her, and bring it to this house?

Mildred was at a loss, but was determined to keep the conversation going. "You're an American, I presume."

"Yes, ma'am. I was born and raised in Texas but I've lived in Scotland for the past several years."

Mildred was becoming desperate. "Oh, then I don't suppose you know my dear friend, Catherine Cromwell? I haven't seen her for years and I must admit that I'm not sure if she said she was moving to Chambury or Tetbury. I really want to get in touch with her."

"No," said David. "But I do know the name. I keep getting mail for her in my mailbox. I sometimes wonder if the chap at the mailbox rental shop can read."

"Oh," said Mildred, "then that must mean she definitely lives in or around Chambury. Thank you so much."

"You're welcome," said David, beginning to feel somewhat ashamed of his lie, "and thank you again for helping Molly."

Mildred had turned to leave when David, gathering his courage, decided to venture into the unknown. "Miss Pankhurst, how long will you be staying in Chambury?"

"I'll be leaving tomorrow – or perhaps the day after. I haven't decided yet."

"Would you consider having dinner with me tonight? I understand that there is an excellent Indian restaurant in the village. Or, if you'd prefer, the King's Inn supposedly serves a first rate traditional English dinner."

"I'd be delighted," said Mildred. "Either place would be fine. I'm staying at the Bashful Badger, in one of their B&B rooms. Why don't you come by at about eight and we can walk to the restaurant from there."

"I'll be there," replied David.

As Mildred walked away, David wondered if he had lost his mind. He had lied to her, but then she had lied to him. David had been watching from a window when the woman had opened the gate, petted Molly on the head, and headed straight for his front door. At no time had she ever removed a thorn from Molly's paw.

She was, however, most definitely the very same "Mildred Pankhurst" with whom his aunt had been corresponding.

#####

Mildred returned to the Bashful Badger to discover that Dylan Jones was still sitting at the same outside table. And he was inhaling yet another pint. As much as she wanted to avoid the man, she still decided to take a seat at the table.

"Ah, Miss Pankhurst, back from your little walk, I see. May I buy you a pint?"

"No thank you, Mr. Jones, I'd just like to ask you a question. Would you happen to know a young woman who either lives in this village or at least somewhere nearby? Her name is Catherine Cromwell."

"No, I'm quite sure that I know of no one by that name. Of course new people, particularly those pushy Londoners, have been moving into the area recently. But, that name isn't one I'm familiar with, I'm afraid."

"Ah; well I believe I'll go to my room now," said Mildred. "I've got several manuscripts to read."

"Before you go," said Dylan, "I think there is something that you should know about the chap that I exchanged greetings with a few minutes ago, the tall Yank and his dog."

"Oh," said Mildred, returning to her seat, "and just why should I need to know anything about him?"

"Well, I did notice that you seemed to be staring at him as he crossed the street. Should you have any interest at all in him, you should know his background. The man is a drunk, unemployed, and – in fact – unemployable. And then there's the fact that he's an American."

Before Mildred could reply, Dylan continued. "Do you recall that terrible pumping station accident near Aberdeen last year? That was caused by that man and it resulted in the death of several men. Furthermore, awful things seem to follow him; the police have only now discovered that his aunt, the poor woman he inherited his house from, was poisoned. He's a man that I'd keep my distance from, if I were you."

#####

Mogilany, Poland; Wednesday, 21 April 2010: Liliana indulged in a typical Polish breakfast consisting of an open-face sandwich, or zapiekanka, plus eggs scrambled with bits of sausage. She finished her meal with a steaming cup of kawa, a type of pot-boiled coffee. It all reminded her of her childhood and the mother and father who were no longer with her.

Putting those memories aside, Liliana left the B&B and walked to the modest house that her driver had pointed out to her the previous day. Reaching the house, she knocked on the door. A moment later a middle-aged woman appeared, dressed entirely in black.

Liliana was taken aback for a moment. The woman was clearly in mourning but Liliana felt compelled to ask her the one question she had traveled so far to pose. "I hope that I'm not imposing, but I'd very much like to talk with Piotr Bartkowski. I understand that he lives here," said Liliana, in her English-accented Polish.

A man appeared in the hallway behind the woman. "When the English come, death follows," he said. "Tell her to go away."

"No, please," said Liliana. "I've come so far and it's extremely important that I speak to Mr. Bartkowski."

The woman nodded, then turned to face the man in the hallway. "I will speak to her. Go to work, you'll be late. Go now!"

The man shrugged, glared for a moment at Liliana, and then brushed past her as he exited the house. "Come in," said the woman. "Come sit."

The woman, who said her name was Katarzyna, pointed to a nearly threadbare sofa while taking a seat on a chair opposite the sofa. "My husband," said Katarzyna, "is very angry. You must excuse him. It is his grandfather, Piotr Bartkowski, that we are mourning. You are too late to talk with him, but I would like to know just why you felt it was so important to do so."

#####

Chambury; Wednesday, 21 April 2010: David reached the front of the Bashful Badger at precisely 8 p.m. Mildred Pankhurst, however, was nowhere to be seen. He stood in front of the pub for a few minutes and then went inside. He then sat at a table for approximately 20 more minutes. Still no sign of the woman.

"Sir," said David to the owner, "do you know if Miss Pankhurst is in her room? I'm supposed to be meeting her for dinner."

The owner, frowning, looked David up and down before replying. "Miss Pankhurst is in her room and asked that she not, under any circumstances, be disturbed."

Chapter 18

Chambury; Thursday, 22 April 2010: David woke to what was becoming a familiar sensation, the tugging on his bedcovers. Molly was clearly anxious to conduct her morning ritual: her toilet, her breakfast, and then a brisk walk into the village.

Once Molly had been fed, David had only to say the word, "walk," for Molly to retrieve her collar and leash. Once those had been secured, David opened the front door and was about to close it behind him when a car came to a sudden stop directly in front of the house. A tall, slender young woman in a police uniform and an older, sour-looking man in civilian clothes – wearing what appeared to be tinted glasses – exited the car.

"Are you Mr. David Wallace?" asked the man.

David nodded in the affirmative.

"Mr. Wallace, we'd like to talk to you with regard to your late aunt's death, if you don't mind. I'm Detective Chief Inspector Grahame and this," he said, pointing to the young policewoman, "is Detective Constable Blake. And this," DCI Grahame added, waving a piece of plastic and badge, "is my warrant card. Why don't we go inside and talk."

"Certainly," said David, holding the front door open.

DCI Grahame took a seat on the sofa in the

drawing room while DC Blake remained standing. David sat in a chair opposite Grahame.

"Mr. Wallace, as I mentioned, we're here to talk to you about your great aunt, Rebecca Fleming. To get to the point, the results of the second autopsy on your aunt indicate that she was evidently poisoned or, at the very least, overmedicated. Traces of Diazepam were found in her system. According to her physician, however, she was not taking Diazepam. In fact, the only medication she had ever prescribed for her was a combination salve and moisturizer."

"Diazepam? Isn't that just Valium, something people use to treat anxiety?" asked David, noticing that the young female DC had left the drawing room and was now in the kitchen.

"It has several uses, so they tell me," DCI Grahame replied. "It can, however, cause serious side effects – including death in the event of an overdose. The side effects of a less than lethal overdose include extreme drowsiness, loss of balance, weakened muscles, disorientation, and fainting. We were informed that your aunt exhibited these side effects in the week preceding her death."

"So I've been told," said David. "But I was also told that the initial autopsy indicated that she had drowned."

"It did, but the drowning could well have been a consequence of the overdose of Diazepam. Your aunt may have been so disoriented that she wandered to the edge of the pond behind this house and then fell in."

David decided not to voice his doubt that his sick, elderly aunt might have been able to make that walk.

"So then, who do you suspect caused my aunt's death?"

"That hasn't yet been determined. I can only say that we have two persons of interest. One, as you might know, is Liliana Kowalski. Would you happen to know where she is at this moment?"

"I have no idea. I barely know the woman."

"She was seen entering your house the evening of April 16th. You were also seen talking to her in the village library. That would seem to indicate that you know her somewhat more than 'barely.'"

"She simply came by on the 16th to tell me how to take care of Molly, my aunt's dog. That was the very first time I had ever met the woman. Our 'meeting' in the library was simply a result of questions I had about some Polish newspaper clippings. She offered to translate them for me."

DCI Grahame simply nodded. DC Tommi Blake, in the meantime, was no where to be seen.

"You said there are *two* persons of interest," said David. "Who might the other one be?"

"That would be you, Mr. Wallace. That would be you."

David Wallace was stunned. "You can't be serious. Up until a few days ago I didn't even know that Rebecca Fleming was my great aunt. In fact, I didn't know the woman even existed. I had never even been to Chambury until my arrival last week. How in the world could you think that I might have had something to do with her death?"

"You are not being accused, Mr. Wallace. You are simply a person of interest. I am here to inform you of that fact and that we would ask you – voluntarily at this time – to provide us with your passport."

"I'll 'voluntarily' provide you with my passport only if you first answer one question. Why would you possibly think that I had anything to do with my aunt's death?"

"Once again, Mr. Wallace," said DCI Grahame, "you are not being accused. If, however, one examines the facts, I believe it's reasonable for you to be classified as a person of interest. Allow me to elaborate. First of all, are you not the same David Wallace whose negligence was blamed for the AXe pumping station tragedy in Scotland last year?"

"I may have been blamed for the accident, but I was certainly not responsible for it. There was, as you must know, no attempt to hold me legally responsible."

"I'm aware of that," said Grahame, "but you were, however, made redundant. Furthermore, you not only lost your job but you have also become, I believe its fair to say, unemployable in your chosen profession. As I understand it, until your aunt's estate was transferred to you, you were virtually penniless. Is that not true?"

"It may be true but, as I told you, I didn't even know who Rebecca Fleming was until last week. Furthermore, until last week I had never ever visited Chambury, or in fact ever been in its vicinity."

"Mr. Wallace, according to our records, you were found asleep in your car on the edge of a slip road just off the M5. That was on 6 April, and that was but 70 miles north of Chambury – and more than 400 miles south of Aberdeen."

"I'm sorry, I have to admit that I had forgotten

about that," David replied, realizing that he had indeed woken up that day, found himself parked on the side of the slip road, with no memory whatsoever as to how he had gotten there.

"Inspector Grahame, I can only give you my word. Sir, I didn't visit Chambury prior to last week; I didn't know I had an aunt here until last week; and I had no reason to do my aunt harm – an aunt I didn't even know existed until last week."

"Mr. Wallace," said DCI Grahame, his voice dripping with sarcasm, "you say you had no reason to do your aunt harm. I would think that inheriting her house and over 300,000 pounds sterling might be considered an incentive. Particularly so if one is unemployed, unemployable, and penniless. Mr. Wallace, one learns as a law enforcement officer to 'always follow the money.' While that may not always hold true, it is something we must consider."

"I can only tell you, once again, that I had nothing to do with my aunt's death, or her decision to include me in her will," David replied, dumbfounded by the turn of events.

"Is that your automobile, the Renault Twingo, parked in front of the house?"

"Yes, why do you ask?"

"DC Blake will need your keys. Once this matter is settled, you may pick up your car at our impound lot in Guyton-upon-Cham. And please do fetch your passport, Mr. Wallace."

When David returned with his passport he discovered that his humiliation had not yet ended.

"Thank you, Mr. Wallace. There is one more thing. I advise you to send, as soon as possible, the rent money you owe on your flat in Aberdeen. If you do that, your landlord has assured me that he will not take legal action."

#####

David watched as DC Blake was finally able to start the Twingo, and continued watching as the young woman drove the car away, trailed by a billowing plume of grey smoke. He then walked back to the drawing room and took a seat on its oversize chair.

He could hardly believe what had just transpired. DCI Grahame may have said that he was "just a person of interest" but his manner, and everything else he had said or implied led David to believe that the man was convinced that David had murdered his aunt.

DCI Grahame's remark about being found in his car only 70 miles north of Chambury was devastating. David could but barely recall that incident but he knew it had happened. It hadn't been the only time that he had woken to find himself somewhere and not having any idea as to how he had gotten there. His drinking, he realized, had been punctuated with blackouts. Still, he could not believe that he had anything to do with his aunt's death.

Then there was the equally disturbing matter of Mildred Pankhurst. He was, he had to admit, in love with the "Thunderbolt" woman. There was, however, no chance whatsoever that she would ever feel the same. He was unemployed, unemployable, and now a "person of interest" in a murder case. It was, he decided, for the best that she had stood him up the previous evening.

David did not move from the chair until more

than two hours later, and then only at the urging of Molly. He attached the leash to her collar and walked to the front door. Once there, he paused, turned, and returned to the drawing room where he had placed the brightly patterned package that he had retrieved from the mailbox rental shop the previous day.

Once they had reached the village, Molly hesitated in front of the butcher shop. Its owner, Frank Owen, appeared with a dog biscuit in hand. The man had a frown on his face as he held out the biscuit. David voiced the "Yes" command to allow Molly to retrieve the biscuit. The twosome then made their way up the street. No words had been exchanged between Frank Owen and David; and David was quite sure why. Nothing in a small village ever remains a secret for long.

David's suspicions were confirmed as he continued down the street. Villagers either averted their eyes as they passed him or, in two instances, stared daggers at him. His reception at the mailbox rental shop was, however, no different than before. The man behind the counter, as usual, turned his back on him. David walked up to the counter and asked for a large manila envelope. After paying for it he placed the contents of the brightly patterned envelope, a thick manuscript, into the new envelope and then placed the now empty envelope in his aunt's mailbox.

He then looked out of the storefront's window. As he had anticipated, there in a second level window above the Bashful Badger was Mildred Pankhurst. She was peering out her bedroom window and, in fact, looking directly at the mailbox rental shop. He knew that the sun was reflected on the shop's window and that, while he could see her, she was unable to see him.

#####

Mildred Pankhurst had been watching the mailbox rental shop for several hours before she saw David Wallace and his dog walking up the street. She watched as the man tied his dog's leash to a metal pole in front of that shop. He then petted the dog on the head and walked into the shop. The dog sat back on her haunches and stared at the door. Once David had closed the door, Mildred was unable to see just what he was doing. She was quite sure, however, that he had been carrying the brightly patterned package that she had sent to Catherine Cromwell.

A few minutes later he exited the shop to the obvious delight of his dog. He was carrying a package, but definitely not the one she had mailed to Catherine Cromwell. Evidently his claim that the package for Catherine had accidently been placed in his mailbox was true. She watched as David untied the dog's leash and the two walked away and out of sight.

Mildred decided to wait a few more hours before checking out of her room and returning to Cheltenham. There was still a chance, she believed, that Catherine Cromwell might retrieve the package she had sent her – allowing Mildred to confront the woman and demand a face-to-face discussion.

As Mildred, her eyes now tired from staring out the window, sat watching, David Wallace and his dog reappeared. They were now on her side of the street. Despite what that man, Dylan Jones, had said about David, she still found it difficult to believe. The man obviously loved his dog, and the dog certainly seemed to return that affection. Animals, Mildred believed with all her heart, were far better judges of people than human beings.

And there was yet another matter that Mildred found quite troubling. She very much liked the man. She was, she had to admit, attracted to him. With that disturbing thought haunting her, she continued to watch the street, hoping that the elusive Catherine Cromwell might soon appear.

Chapter 19

Guyton-upon-Cham; Thursday, 22 April 2010: DC Tommi Blake struggled to keep the Renault Twingo on the road. The wreck of a car made the winding road from Chambury to Guyton-upon-Cham an even more difficult drive than usual. Adding to her anxiety was her growing concern as to the behavior of DCI Grahame.

Grahame had ordered her to conduct a surreptitious inspection of David Wallace's house while the man was distracted by Grahame's interview. He had not, however, made any effort to request a search warrant, arguing that an officer had the right to "simply walk around" a suspect's or person of interest's home without the need for such a warrant. While his argument may have been technically correct, it could have a negative impact on the villagers' view of the police.

Tommi was also concerned that Grahame had revealed far too much of what the police knew of David Wallace's activities, particularly the matter of his being found asleep on a M5 slip road just 70 miles from Chambury. Tommi, herself, would not have revealed that fact until David Wallace was arrested, cautioned, and interrogated.

Those matters, however, paled in comparison to Grahame's insistence on labeling Liliana Kowalski as a "person of interest." The woman had *voluntarily* provided Tommi with a sugar bowl she had taken from Rebecca Fleming's house. She had even asked that the residue on the bowl be tested. The lab results had revealed that the residual was Diazepam – and that the *only* fingerprints on the bowl belonged to Liliana.

Grahame ignored Tommi's explanation for the fingerprints found on the bowl. What else, Tommi had asked, would one expect as it was Liliana who had picked up the bowl and brought it to Tommi at HQ. That argument had fallen on deaf ears and now Liliana Kowalski had fled, making it seem even more likely – at least to the hard-headed Inspector Grahame – that she had poisoned or overmedicated her closest friend.

The matter, however, that truly angered Tommi was the fact that, even though *she* had found out about David Wallace being fired by AXe, and of his being discovered asleep on the slip road, and the late night visit to his house by Liliana, DCI Grahame had asked PC Billy Milne to continue that portion of the investigation.

Tommi, for her part, argued that there should be an investigation of Dylan Jones. Jones, Tommi pointed out, certainly had the opportunity to place the Diazepam into Rebecca Fleming's sugar bowl. Grahame, his face turning red, had told her that, while Dylan Jones may have had the opportunity, it was Liliana Kowalski that had the motive – believing she was the heir to the Fleming estate.

Grahame had then warned her to not, under any circumstances, waste the department's scarce resources into any investigation of Dylan Jones. Tommi was becoming more and more convinced that Grahame had, at best, a low opinion of female police officers.

Tommi considered confronting Grahame, or even the station's superintendent. She then thought better of it and attempted to focus on something else – that "something" being the matter of who caused the death of Rebecca Fleming. While Liliana *might* have contributed to the woman's death, Tommi considered that a long shot. And, while it was David Wallace who had everything to gain from his great aunt's death, the man was either a fabulous actor or truly had not committed the crime.

Why, thought Tommi, would someone go to the trouble of adding finely ground Diazepam tablets to Rebecca Fleming's sugar bowl rather than just giving her one deadly dose of the drug? It did, after all, come in liquid form. Someone, she decided, wanted Rebecca to die *slowly*. If David Wallace wanted his aunt dead, or if Liliana sought the same goal, wouldn't either of them have wanted it to be accomplished as fast as possible?

Chapter 20

Cheltenham; Thursday Evening, 22 April 2010: Mildred arrived back at her flat to a mixed reception from Rupert. Initially he nipped at her ankles. Then he produced a ferocious– at least for a cat his size – meow. Rupert was not at all pleased with having been left on his own for two days.

He only calmed down once Mildred picked him up. As she did, she noticed a large manila envelope lying on the floor next to the door's mail slot. It was addressed to the Passionate Word Literary Agency and, Mildred assumed, had been delivered to her flat by someone at the agency.

Mildred took a seat at the kitchen table and, still holding Rupert, opened the package. It was, to her delight, from Catherine Cromwell. The typed note accompanying the manuscript simply read: "*A Cotswold Diary* is finished. I hope it meets your expectations."

Strange wording, thought Mildred. In the past Catherine Cromwell's note had always been much chattier – and far less formal. Furthermore, her correspondence had always been handwritten.

Mildred skimmed through the first 36 chapters. She had only cited a few typos and misspellings in that portion of the manuscript and Catherine had corrected those. What she wanted to read, and desperately so, were the concluding chapters of the book.

Mildred finished reading the now completed story some two hours later. She was simultaneously delighted and confused. She was elated with the fresh, new approach Catherine had employed to rescue the heroine and conclude the book. The writing itself, however, seemed somehow different from the style Mildred had grown accustomed to in Catherine's previous books. Mildred couldn't quite put her finger on it, but she felt that there was a definite, albeit subtle, difference.

Perhaps, she thought, it's my imagination. Then, whether I am imagining things or not, the book is superb. It could be, and should be, the breakthrough novel that should send the young Miss Catherine Cromwell to the very top of the mountain – an increasingly larger mountain – of romance novelists.

Mildred intended to take tomorrow's train to London and meet with the publisher of Catherine's novels. First, however, she was determined to find out just where Catherine Cromwell lived – and just why the talented young woman was so intent on remaining hidden from the public eye.

Chambury; Thursday Evening, 22 April 2010: David sat in the kitchen, watching the water dripping from its leaky tap. He had intended to fix that but, after the events of today, decided to purchase a bottle of Scotch Whiskey – Royal Lochnagar 12 years old. He had managed to find a glass and open the bottle when he noticed that Molly was watching him.

Perhaps it was his imagination but the dog appeared to be giving him an accusatory look. David grabbed the bottle, got up, and poured its 50 pound sterling's worth of contents down the kitchen sink's drain.

"All right, Molly, stop looking at me like that. Let's go upstairs; I've got an idea how to best spend the evening. In fact, I've even got a title for it. Molly, I'm going to call it *Colpo di Fulmine*. In case you don't understand Italian, Molly, that means *Thunderbolt*. As long as I'm a 'person of interest' I might as well do something to pass the time."

Chapter 21

Cheltenham; Friday Morning, 23 April 2010: Mildred had often admired the elegant stone building that housed the offices of Dorrit and Dombey but had never ventured inside. Dorrit and Dombey, it was well known, was a highly regarded investment firm. Mildred, at least at this stage in her life, had nothing to invest. The rent for her apartment, food for herself and Rupert, care of her car, and the purchase of an occasional new item of clothing consumed the bulk of the income she received from the Passionate Word Literary Agency.

Today, however, she was determined to enter the imposing doors of Dorrit and Dombey and unwrap the mystery named Catherine Cromwell. For years, Catherine's royalties, less the 15 per cent fee charged by the Passionate Word Literary Agency, had been sent to Dorrit and Dombey rather than directly to Catherine Cromwell. Mildred's inspection of Catherine's file, beginning with the very first piece of correspondence she had ever sent the agency, revealed that at no time in the initial correspondence had she ever revealed a mailing address other than Dorrit and Dombey, and – only later – the rental box in Chambury. Mildred could only hope that someone at Dorrit and Dombey would provide the address of the place in which she actually lived.

The interior of the Dorrit and Dombey building was even more impressive than its exterior. Mildred had never seen so much mahogany in her life. Even the receptionist's desk was solid mahogany. Mildred had the distinct impression that she had, somehow, been transformed back to the 19th century.

The receptionist informed Mildred that Mr. Dombey was running a few minutes late and that their 9:30 a.m. meeting would not start until roughly 9:45. Mildred thanked the receptionist and took a seat in reception area. There was but one other person in the area, an elderly woman who appeared to be dozing.

At approximately 9:50 a.m. a young man left the office of Andrew Dombey and the receptionist gave Mildred a wave. "You may go in now, Miss Pankhurst. Mr. Dombey will see you now but remember that he can only spare a few minutes."

#####

"Mr. Dombey, my name is Mildred Pankhurst. I'm an agent at the Passionate Word Literary Agency. In fact, we are neighbors. Our offices are in a building just a few doors down. I really want to thank you for making time for me this morning."

"That's quite all right, Miss Pankhurst. After all, it is the neighborly thing to do. Now, according to what our receptionist tells me, you are inquiring about Catherine Cromwell. Is that right?"

"Yes, that's correct. Mr. Dombey, it's very important that I meet, face-to-face, with Miss Cromwell. I'm her agent and I know that all her financial matters have always been directed to your offices. But, Mr. Dombey, the only contact I have with her is by means of mail – and that mail is being delivered to a mailbox rental shop in Chambury. Sir, would it be possible for you to provide me with her home address, or perhaps even a phone number? I can assure you that this involves a matter of utmost importance, both for her and myself."

"Miss Pankhurst, I'm terribly sorry but I cannot divulge that information without the explicit permission of Miss Cromwell. I doubt very much … in fact I'm positive that she will not grant that permission."

"I can't say that I'm not disappointed, but I understand. There is one other question that I have; is Catherine Cromwell her real name? Or is that simply her pen name?"

Andrew Dombey hesitated before answering. "I'm afraid that I cannot answer that question either. I'm truly sorry."

Mildred left the offices of Dorrit and Dombey and walked back to those of the Passionate Word Literary Agency. While she had not held out much hope that Andrew Dombey would reveal any information with regard to Catherine Cromwell, she was almost positive that he had – by his pause before replying to her question about a pen name – revealed the fact that Catherine Cromwell was indeed a pen name.

#####

Mildred arrived, by taxi, at the Cheltenham Spa train station just in time to board the train to London's Paddington Station. She spent most of the three-plus hours on the train *trying* to think about what to say to Emily Arlington, the romance novel editor at Hull and Cooper. Her thoughts, however, kept returning to a man she hardly knew, David Wallace.

Mildred took a taxi to meet Emily at her friend's favorite restaurant, the Wolseley on Piccadilly. Emily Arlington and Mildred Pankhurst had known each other since their school days. Once they graduated university, however, they had taken two rather different paths. Emily had joined the Hull and Cooper publishing house and quickly rose to a senior editor position. Mildred had turned down an offer with a large literary agency in London and joined Passionate Word.

"Well, Mildred," said Emily, "how is Laurence?"

"Laurence is history."

"Why's that? No, wait, let me guess. Rupert didn't like him."

"Rupert *hated* him."

"Mildred, does your definition of the perfect man include the requirement that he must like cats?"

"Laugh if you will," Mildred replied, "but you can tell a lot about a person on the basis of how he or she treats animals."

"I suppose so, but I'm beginning to believe that the man you are looking for is a cat-loving Mr. Darcy straight out of a Jane Austen novel. Mildred, you've got to stop reading *Pride and Prejudice*. There is, my dear, no such thing as a perfect man."

"Yes," said Mildred, thinking of David Wallace, "every time you think you've found one, you discover that he is either allergic to cat dander or has a rather disconcerting past. But that's not why I'm here. I've brought you a finished copy of Catherine Cromwell's novel, *A Cotswold Diary*. It's the one that we discussed about a month or so ago."

"I remember our discussion. I'll read it tonight.

But, tell me, why did the Cromwell woman take so awfully long to finish it? Mildred, while the books I edit have to be well-written, you've got to realize that we thrive on volume. I'm not sure that your Catherine Cromwell can produce her works fast enough. Some of my best-selling romance novelists are turning out a book a month and a few are even faster. A romance novelist has to keep her name out there, and that means she must write rapidly. If not, her audience is going to seek out other authors. I'm afraid that some readers have a short attention span."

"I understand that, Emily, but you said that *A Cotswold Diary*, even the unfinished portion you read, would make a wonderful movie."

"I said that and I stand by it. But let me read the finished manuscript before we decide on how to handle that matter. On a related topic, have you been able to convince Miss Cromwell to do something, anything, to help promote her novels?"

"No, but I'm still holding out hope," Mildred replied.

Mildred returned to Cheltenham on the 8:45 p.m. train out of Paddington Station, arriving in Cheltenham a few minutes after 11 p.m. Rupert was, as usual, a bit cross at her late arrival and refused, for about five minutes, to allow her to pick him up. He was, she decided, almost as difficult to deal with as Catherine Cromwell, or whatever the obstinate woman's real name might be.

Chapter 22

Chambury; Saturday Morning, 24 April 2010: David was woken by Molly at precisely 7:00 a.m. "Molly, can't you give a guy a break? I just spent nearly ten hours straight writing. Do we really have to get up this early?"

Molly simply tugged harder on David's bedcovers.

Once Molly had been fed, David was determined to take a break from writing. The *Thunderbolt* novel would have to wait. He decided to go for a drive in the country. While the police had taken his old car, they were evidently unaware of the shiny white Vauxhall Astra that was parked in the shed in the back garden.

"Molly, why don't we see just what the countryside around here looks like?"

The dog gave David a puzzled look but eagerly followed him to the shed. Once David had opened the shed door, and then the driver's side door on the Astra, he stood to one side. Molly, tail wagging wildly, leapt into the car and positioned herself on the passenger side seat. She then gave David a look that seemed, at least to David, to say: Let's get this show on the road!

David took the long and winding road out of the village, through Guyton-upon-Cham, to the A433, and then to its intersection with the A429, and headed north. That's when he noticed a green Range Rover traveling behind him. It had long been David's dream to own a new Range Rover although, even when he was employed, there would have been no way for him to afford the 90,000 pounds sterling beauty. And most certainly not considering the spending habits and expensive tastes of his ex-wife.

David's first stop was the picturesque village of Bourton-on-the-Water. While it was a rather touristy destination, David wanted to visit its Cotswold Motoring Museum. A pleasant hour or so later, he and Molly were off again. As he once again headed north on the A429, he noticed that there was a green Range Rover following him – quite possibly the very same car he had seen earlier that day. The Range Rover was close enough for David to make out the driver. It was a man, a very large man.

About 10 minutes later David decided to visit the market village of Stow-on-the-Wold. He parked the Astra in the market square and he and Molly investigated the village church, a lovely Norman edifice. They then walked around the village, stopping at several shops and concluding their visit with a treat at the village bakery.

There was, David realized, a distinct difference between the villages he had visited that day and the far more sedate – and isolated – village of Chambury. The villages of Bourton-on-the-Water, Stow-on-the-Wold, and several others in the Cotswold region of Gloucestershire were tourism magnets, attracting tens of thousands of visitors each year. Both Bourton and Stow were easily accessible via A-roads. Chambury, on the other hand, could only be reached by a narrow, winding B-road.

If, however, he had to choose between living in the touristy towns of the Cotswolds and Chambury, there was no doubt in his mind. He would prefer Chambury.

David decided it was time to return to Chambury and continue his writing. He and Molly got into the Astra and drove south. In his rear view mirror, David saw the very same green Range Rover that had followed him to Stow.

He wondered if it might be the local police, following him in an unmarked car. Whoever it was in the Range Rover, however, had definitely been following David.

David arrived at the Fleming house shortly after 6 p.m. The green Range Rover had stopped following him once he had entered Chambury.

David decided to continue writing the *Thunderbolt* novel, hoping that might take his mind off of his present situation. Not only was he a "person of interest" in his aunt's death, he was now being followed by a strange man in a green Range Rover.

Chapter 23

Mogilany, Poland; Saturday, 24 April 2010: Liliana sat in the lobby of her B&B, her mind virtually awhirl with questions and concerns. Should she go back to England? If so, should she take a ferry this time? While she had managed to slip into France and ultimately Poland without a problem, would it be that easy to return home? There would be, she realized, the need to go through both French exit checks as well as UK passport checks at the Calais ferry terminal. Were the police looking for her? Liliana did know one person who might be able to answer at least some of her questions: Joyce Blake, her assistant at the Chambury library.

Liliana placed a call to Joyce, who answered on the first ring. "Miss Kowalski, I've been so worried about you. Where are you?"

"Hello, Joyce," Liliana replied. "I'd rather not say where I am at the moment. All I can say is that I'm not in the UK and I'm trying to determine whether or not to return. Have you talked to your sister, Tommi? What might she know about my situation?"

"Tommi tells me that the death of Miss Fleming has been determined to be a *possible* homicide. They are still working on the case but the preliminary ruling is that she was murdered. Detective Chief Inspector Grahame has listed two individuals as persons of interest. You, Miss Kowalski, are one and the other is David Wallace."

"Mr. Wallace is a 'person of interest?' How in the world can that be? The last time the man saw Rebecca was more than a quarter century ago."

"I really don't know why either of you are considered persons of interest. All that Tommi would tell me was that they have talked to Mr. Wallace and want, very much, to talk to you. The police have, by the way, searched your flat and secured its entrance. Miss Kowalski, if you do return you won't be able to get into your flat without first going to the police."

After completing her phone call to Joyce, Liliana decided to first visit her parents' graves, and then risk a return ferry trip to England. If I am, she thought, just a "person of interest," then perhaps it would be safe to return to England.

Guyton-upon-Cham; Saturday, 24 April 2010: Detective Constable Tommi Blake had looked forward to her assignment in the investigation into the death of Miss Rebecca Fleming. This was her opportunity to work with Detective Chief Investigator Keith Grahame, a man with a reputation for his ability to solve crimes. But Tommi now questioned that notion. She was convinced that Dylan Jones, the executor of Rebecca's estate, should be considered a suspect. Despite that, DCI Grahame did not share her opinion.

In fact, the man had the audacity to give her an impromptu tutorial on what he considered to be the very key to being a successful detective.

"Blake, if you are to ever make Chief Inspector, you need to realize that, in this business, we are almost always faced with the problem of scarce resources. In the case of Guyton-upon-Cham, there are even scarcer resources – not enough people, not enough money. In a murder investigation you mustn't waste those resources, or your time, on anything other than those potential suspects that have both *means* and *motive*. The motive in virtually all murders is either revenge or money. I think we can rule out revenge in this case; that leaves money as the motive …'

"But, sir," said Tommi, hoping to voice an objection.

"Damn it, Blake, don't interrupt. Listen and learn, listen and learn.

"As I was trying to say, money is definitely the motive in this case. Liliana Kowalski thought she was going to inherit the Fleming estate; therefore she had a motive. David Wallace *did* inherit the estate, and thus he must be considered to have a motive. Dylan Jones, on the other hand, was simply the estate's executor, knew who would inherit the estate, and yet received nothing other than a small fee. Furthermore, our check of Rebecca Fleming's accounts – and the contents of her house – show that Dylan Jones did not profit, not one iota, from the death of Rebecca Fleming. Do not, Blake, waste your time on any investigation of Dylan Jones.

"The other thing that a detective must do is to learn everything possible *about the victim*. What I want you to do, Blake, is to explore the background of Rebecca Fleming. Learn everything you possibly can about the woman."

Tommi couldn't believe it. DCI Grahame had claimed that only Liliana Kowalski and David Wallace had a motive; yet he was asking her to investigate the victim rather than find the perpetrator of the crime. It was all, thought Tommi Blake, frustrating as well as a waste of her time.

#####

Lord Emsworth's Manor House, Chambury; Saturday, 24 April 2010: Reginald Emsworth, or "Lord Emsworth" as he demanded to be addressed, sat in his wheelchair on the balcony directly behind his stately home's study. Reginald Emsworth would reach the ripe old age of 90 in a matter of weeks. He had been born the son of a humble Chambury shopkeeper but had, in his first 27 years, fought his way to the achievement of the life of a wealthy and respected man. He credited his success to his sheer determination, coupled with – he had to admit – a fair amount of luck.

Now, as he was closing in on the end of his life, his luck seemed to be changing. "Lady" Charlotte, his lovely and much younger wife, was spending more and more time in London and less and less with him. In fact, he was beginning to see more of his third wife in photos on the pages of British tabloids rather than in their Cotswold manor.

His only child, Henry, was and always had been a disappointment. He had been a shy, introverted child and had grown into an overly large, awkward, and introverted man. Henry had yet to marry and Lord Emsworth suspected that he never would. His son seemed incapable of doing anything right, as Lord Emsworth had first discovered some thirty years ago when he allowed Henry to direct the design, construction, and location of his father's statue – a statue that was to be placed in front of the Chambury library.

Lord Emsworth had been in South Africa during the period. When he returned he saw, to his horror, that his statue was holding a *British Enfield rifle*. His escape from the Nazi death march, however, had been enabled by the seizing of a *German* Mauser-Werke rifle. Had not his dim-witted son read his memoir?

Then there was Henry's fascination with expensive watches. Despite having a drawer full of new or nearly new Rolex, Cartier, and Patek Phillipe timepieces, he had just that week purchased a Rotonde de Cartier Astrotourbilon that likely cost more than his new, specially equipped Range Rover. The boy, thought Lord Emsworth, is a fool for expensive watches and luxury cars.

But perhaps his biggest disappointment thus far had been his misplaced confidence in Dylan Jones. The man had assured him that Rebecca Fleming's house would be his by no later than the end of April. The chance of that promise being kept was becoming less and less likely.

Lord Emsworth did not like, and certainly did not trust Dylan Jones. Unfortunately, there seemed to be no other way to gain possession of Rebecca Fleming's house.

Chapter 24

Guyton-upon-Cham; Sunday, 25 April 2010: Despite the fact that Sunday was usually one of Tommi Blake's days off, she was sitting in DCI Grahame's office and using his computer. The whereabouts of Grahame, himself, was anyone's guess. Tommi's research into the background of Miss Rebecca Fleming – as demanded by DCI Grahame – had produced an unexpected result.

Tommi and her sister, Joyce, had been born and raised in Chambury. Both had known Rebecca Fleming as a somewhat reserved but kindly woman who spent a great deal of time in the village library. Miss Fleming had arrived in Chambury 25 years ago after purchasing what had come to be known as "the Fleming house." To Tommi's knowledge, the woman's only close friend was Liliana Kowalski.

The only thing even remotely unusual about Rebecca Fleming were the scars on the back of her hands, often covered or at least partially covered by the wearing of long-sleeved blouses and, on occasion, white gloves. She also had a slight scarring of her forehead and, according to Tommi's interview of her physician – a woman in Cheltenham – had undergone some facial reconstruction. Rebecca had refused, however, to reveal the cause of her scaring and plastic surgery to her doctor.

The Cheltenham physician claimed that Rebecca Fleming was in excellent, if not remarkable, physical condition and that her biological age was that of a woman at least a decade younger. The only prescriptions she had written for her, during the entire 28 years she had served as her physician, were salves and ointments for the relief of the discomfort caused by her scars. Those facts appeared to rule out any likelihood that Rebecca Fleming had *knowingly* overdosed on Diazepam – or even had access to the drug.

Tommi had been able to determine that Rebecca had been employed as a secretary, for the law firm of Allerton and Fawcett in Cheltenham, for the three years immediately prior to her move to Chambury. Prior to that position, she had worked – again as a secretary – for the now defunct book publishing firm of Walpole and Stuart in London. She had been employed in that position for seven years, starting on 14 March of 1975.

And it was there that Tommi Blake's search ended in frustration. Rebecca Fleming seemed to have somehow appeared from out of thin air in London. There was no record of any previous employment – or addresses – prior to 1975. There was only a record of a passport, first issued in 1974. However, the address listed on that first passport did not and never had existed.

Tommi had also conducted a search of anyone within the UK having the same name and birthdate as claimed by Rebecca Fleming. She found just one person, a female infant who had been born in Yorkshire on 7 March 1926 and had died on 9 March that same year.

So, thought Tommi, the seemingly unremarkable, elderly woman that everyone had known as Miss Rebecca Fleming had evidently taken on the identity of a child who died 84 years ago. It seemed more than likely that Chambury's Rebecca Fleming was a woman in hiding – from someone or something.

While Tommi felt that this new information was remarkable, she had yet to determine how it might provide a clue as to the person or persons who had murdered Rebecca Fleming. And how, she wondered, did David Wallace fit into this puzzle?

#####

Chambury; Sunday, 25 April 2010: For what seemed like the hundredth time, David tossed the brand new but now soggy tennis ball to the far edge of his rear garden. Molly, her tail wagging like an out-of-control helicopter rotor blade, raced after it. The delighted dog retrieved the ball and sprinted back to David, eager to continue the game.

"Molly, old girl, let's take a break. I don't know about you but my shoulder hurts. How about we take a nice walk to the pond? I'm sure you'll find something interesting there like frogs, salamanders, or – if we're lucky – maybe even some ducks."

David first considered sitting in the grass at the edge of the pond before noticing that, on the far side of the pond, there was a footpath and, along side it, a wooden bench. He took a seat there while Molly investigated, in painstaking detail, the flora and fauna surrounding the pond. Thank goodness, thought David, that Molly doesn't know that this is where her mistress perished.

Some 20 minutes later, Molly, evidently finished with her exploration, decided to join David. She insisted on lying next to him on the bench, her head resting on his lap.

David could only wonder if the gentle animal "loved" him, in the sense applied to a human's concept of love. She certainly seemed content – particularly so when they went for walks or the occasional drive. Best of all, she was spending less time at the front gate.

The only thing he knew, for certain, was that he had formed a strong attachment to the dog. She slept close to his side every night. He didn't even really mind it when she got up early and tugged on his bedcovers. Molly, the sad-eyed yellow Lab, was not only David's best friend; she was – he realized – his only friend.

Suddenly David felt Molly's body tense. The dog leapt to the ground, her body now rigid and head pointed in the direction of the high grass on the far side of the meadow that separated the bench from a small, solitary stone cottage.

There, walking toward David and Molly, was a man wearing a Harris Tweed jacket and matching flat cap. He was using a walking stick to assist his hike through the tall grass and was now waving at David with his free hand.

Molly, her ears up, tail held high and wagging from side to side, suddenly let out a series of short, excited outbursts. Then she raced, at top speed, toward the approaching man.

David was stunned. Never before had Molly showed even a hint of aggression toward anyone. Yet she appeared to be intent on attacking the man with the walking stick. David feared for the man's safety and, even more, for that of Molly. A walking stick could prove to be a deadly weapon in the hands of a man intent on defending himself from an attacking dog.

David was about to shout for Molly to stop when a small animal suddenly appeared from out of the tall grass. It was a cat, a cat as black as coal and with luminous yellow eyes. The cat was racing toward Molly, seemingly on a collision course with the much larger animal.

Both animals put on the brakes and came to a stop when but a few inches apart. The cat then leapt toward Molly, wrapping his front legs around the dog's neck. The black cat, David suddenly realized, was *hugging* Molly. The cat was, in fact, purring.

"Winston has dearly missed his visits with Molly," said the man. "It's good to see them at play again. I'm your neighbor, Miles Shrewsbury, from across the way," added the man, pointing to the small stone cottage on the far side of the meadow. "I assume that you are Mr. Wallace, Miss Fleming's nephew?"

"Yes, I'm David Wallace, pleased to meet you Mr. Shrewsbury," said David, still unable to take his eyes off of Molly, the yellow Lab, and Winston, the cat. "Got to admit that I've never seen anything like that before," he added, pointing to Molly and Winston, who were now grooming one another.

"They've always played together like that. They were, after all, raised together. More like brother and sister than cat and dog, I've always said."

"Molly and Winston were raised together?"

"Yes, my wife – that would be Maggie – and I raised them both. Molly was found abandoned beside a road. She was just a tiny bundle of dirty, wet fur when we found her. I really didn't think she would make it.

"Winston, on the other hand, just appeared one day at the front door of our cottage. Poor little fellow couldn't have been more than a couple months old at the time. We took them both in; that was about five years ago. Your aunt saw Molly a few months after we took her in and fell in love with her. She wanted to buy Molly but I told her that, if she promised to take good care of Molly, and let her see Winston once in a while, then Molly was hers. I do hope that their friendship will continue, Mr. Wallace."

"I'd like to see it continue," said David, "but, as you may be aware, I can't guarantee just what might be in my future."

"I imagine you're talking about that 'person of interest' matter that the police have brought up. Yes, I suppose that does cloud one's future, but, Mr. Wallace, you don't look like a murderer to me. I trust Molly's instincts far more than those of the police. Our dear Molly seems to have taken quite a liking to you."

"Well, thank you for your vote of confidence. I just hope that the police will ultimately agree with your assessment."

"Oh, I have no doubt that they'll find out who really murdered your aunt. She was a dear, sweet woman ... a little different and quite reserved until you got to know her ... but still a wonderful person."

"I suppose you knew her well," said David.

"My wife and I have known her for about 25 years. We met her shortly after she moved here from Cheltenham. I have, in fact, been caring for the trees, plants, and bushes in her gardens ever since she moved here."

"Well," said David, "from what I've seen you've done an excellent job. I really admire those hydrangeas – and that flowering bush near the shed although I cannot for the life of me guess just what it might be."

"Ah, that would be an *Illicium Simonsii*. Rebecca asked me to plant it two years ago. It comes from China and is very rare. I gave it little chance of surviving in our climate but it seems to be thriving. Have you noticed its flowers? Lovely pale yellow star-like things. They're blooming now, I do believe. Your aunt truly loved that plant."

David was now only barely listening to the man. He wanted to change the subject to a matter of far more interest to him. "Any idea," asked David, "as to who might have wanted to harm her?"

"Mr. Wallace, until a few weeks before her death, I would have thought that no one would want to do her harm. She did, however, mention something to me after she returned from her holiday in France a month or so ago. It was odd. Rebecca asked that Maggie and I watch her house. She also asked old Mr. Lancaster, from across the street, to keep an eye on things."

"Mr. Lancaster?" said David. "Are you talking about the old fellow in the house directly across the road from my aunt's home, the man who seems to be staring out of an upper story window all the time?"

"That's the one. Mr. Lancaster has insomnia …

hardly ever sleeps. The poor man is confined to his bedroom. Seems to always be looking out that window. Couldn't ask for a better watchman."

"Why," asked David, "did my aunt want you and Mr. Lancaster to watch her house?"

"She said that she was afraid that someone might be wanting to break-in. I asked her why she thought that but she just changed the subject. Then, about a week later, I found her body in the pond."

"You found her? I didn't know that," said David. "Mr. Shrewsbury, do you remember what she was wearing when you found her?"

"As I recall, it was a nightgown, a flannel nightgown. Had pink flower blossoms on it, I do believe. Why do you ask?"

"Just curious," replied David, deciding to change the subject. "On another matter, would you happen to know why my aunt was so interested in Poland?"

"Mr. Wallace, I never knew that your aunt had *any* interest in Poland. She would pass the time of day with me and the wife out here on the bench; but – to tell the truth – she was a bit secretive. That reminds me, have you checked her hiding place, the little wall safe behind that painting of King George VI in her drawing room?"

"No, I must admit to have been totally unaware of any hiding place. How do you know about it?"

"I built it for her, about two years ago. I sometimes did odd jobs for her, as well as maintaining the gardens, and one day she asked me to construct a hiding place behind the painting of King George. If you like, I can show you."

Miles Shrewsbury and David, with Molly and

Winston in close pursuit, walked back to the house, entered through the rear door, and all four found their way to the drawing room.

"So that's supposed to be George VI; I had assumed that it was just a painting of some wall-eyed old guy with a terrific headache," said David.

"No, that's just a particularly poor rendition of him. Despite that, Rebecca said she wanted it placed in front of the hiding place. She said the painting was so awful that nobody would want to steal it. I can assure you, Mr. Wallace, that our King was much better looking than that."

Miles removed the painting and handed it to David. "Bloody hell," said Miles, "someone has broken into the wall safe."

David took in the scene before him. The "wall safe" that Miles Shrewsbury had installed was simply a rectangular hole in the wall. Its opening was "protected" by nothing more than a crude wooden door, a door that had gouge marks on its edges.

"Someone broke into Rebecca's hiding place," said Miles, once again stating the obvious.

The man then pulled the hiding place door away from the wall. The wooden box behind the mangled door was empty.

"Nothing," said Miles, "absolutely nothing in there. Someone broke into Rebecca's hiding place and took everything."

"Any idea of what might have been hidden there?" asked David.

"No, no idea at all. I guessed she wanted to hide some jewelry, or money, but she never said what she wanted to hide. Whatever it was, it's gone now."

Once Miles Shrewsbury had left, David took a seat on the drawing room's oversized chair. He attempted to make sense of the situation. Having excluded alcohol from his diet, he felt that he was finally thinking more clearly. He restrained his initial urge to call the police. That, he decided, would do no good.

It could, in fact, prove particularly troublesome for his neighbor across the meadow. If he told the police that the very same man that discovered Rebecca Fleming's body knew where a "hiding place" was in his late aunt's house, and that it had been broken into, he guessed that they would add a third "person of interest" to their list: Miles Shrewsbury.

Chapter 25

Chambury; Monday, 26 April 2010: Despite the chilly reception David had received during his most recent walks through the village, he had no intention of remaining in his house – or denying Molly her daily "circuit." Shortly after 9 a.m. he and Molly set off on a brisk walk.

David tied Molly's leash to the iron post in front of the mailbox rental shop and prepared to enter. Before he could do so, however, an obviously distraught Mildred Pankhurst burst out of the shop and rushed past David. It all happened so fast that David doubted that Mildred had even noticed him.

David paused at the entrance to the shop, argued with himself for a few seconds, and then turned to watch Mildred race up the street and toward the village bakeshop. He untied Molly's leash and followed Mildred. Despite being stood up by the woman the previous Wednesday, he still wanted to try, one last time, to talk with her – even though he was at a loss as to what to say.

Mildred Pankhurst had taken a seat at an outdoor table in front of the bakeshop, her back to the approach of David and Molly. Even still, David could see from her posture that the woman was upset.

"Miss Pankhurst, may I buy you a cup of coffee and a raisin scone?"

Mildred turned to face David. At first she considered asking the man to leave her alone. She settled, however, on a quite different response. "Yes, I'd love a coffee and scone. You can leave your dog with me, I promise to be good to her."

David reappeared a few minutes later with a tray containing two coffees and a raisin scone. "Miss Pankhurst, we came close to colliding in front of the mailbox rental shop a few minutes ago. Is everything all right? The shop owner isn't the friendliest person in the world and that's probably a massive understatement. Miss Pankhurst, did he upset you?"

"Mr. Wallace, that shop owner is a horrid man! I simply asked him for a description of Catherine Cromwell, the young woman that – as I mentioned to you, last week – I'm looking for. The man just glared at me. Then I pulled out a 50-pound note, laid it on the counter, and asked him to please describe the woman who picked up Catherine Cromwell's mail. He told me to get out and then turned his back on me."

David was surprised. He would have guessed that the surly shop owner would have taken the bribe – and was rather pleased that he hadn't.

"Miss Pankhurst, you told me that Catherine Cromwell was an old friend of yours. Why then, do you need a description?"

"Mr. Wallace," Mildred replied, "I'm afraid that I didn't tell you the truth. The truth of the matter is, however, a long story."

"Molly and I have time for a long story; please do tell it. And please call me David, if you would."

"All right, David, and call me Mildred. But, before I tell you about Catherine Cromwell, I want to apologize for last week. What I did was inexcusable … and cowardly."

"Miss Pankhurst … Mildred," said David, "I'm guessing that you heard the local gossip about me. I have to admit that some of it is true, but before I attempt to explain myself, please tell me more about the Catherine Cromwell matter."

"All right, but remember that I warned you that it is a long – and strange – story. First of all, I have never set eyes on Catherine Cromwell. I'm not even sure that's her real name. You see, I'm a literary agent. I work for the Passionate Word Literary Agency in Cheltenham. I represent authors of romance novels. The woman who calls herself Catherine Cromwell is one of my clients, quite possibly my most promising client. She, however, is unlike any author I've ever dealt with. The woman refuses to meet with me. Our *only* communication is by means of the post. I send my correspondence to her via post – to a mailbox in Chambury's mailbox rental shop. She, in turn, mails everything to me at my agency.

"Last week I sent her a manuscript, one enclosed in a large envelope with a bright checkerboard pattern. When I saw you walking out of the mailbox rental shop with that package I assumed you were taking it to Catherine. I followed you and knocked on the front door of your house, thinking that she lived there. You said she didn't but, to make sure you were telling the truth, I watched the mailbox shop from my room above the Bashful Badger. I saw you return the package on Thursday and realized that it had, just as you said, simply been put in the wrong mailbox – in your mailbox rather than that of Catherine

Cromwell."

At that moment, Mildred paused to take a sip of coffee. David considered telling her the truth about Catherine Cromwell, and his role in misleading her, but quickly dismissed that idea. Mildred Pankhurst already had a bad enough impression of him; he didn't want to add to that.

"Today I was hoping I could find out where she lived, or her real name, from the mailbox rental shop. That, as I mentioned, didn't work out. David, I want so much to give Catherine Cromwell the good news."

"Good news? What good news?"

"I received a call last night. Catherine has been offered a fantastic opportunity. They want to make a movie of her latest book. It's a wonderful novel titled *A Cotswold Diary*. David, they want to make a movie, for television, of *A Cotswold Diary*! I wanted to see her face when I told her that; however it would seem that I'll have to inform her by mail."

"Well," said David, "that still sounds like great news. The woman should still be pleased even if she only learns about it by mail. Besides, perhaps this Catherine Cromwell person has a reason to hide her true identity."

"David, I can't think of one good reason for Catherine Cromwell to refuse to meet with me. Not one."

"Well," said David, "Let me try to think of some. What if the woman is in prison? What if she is not in prison but has committed some horrible crime? What if she is in hiding because someone, maybe an ex-husband or boyfriend, is after her?"

"I've got to admit that those *might* be good reasons.

Still, I think she is just being obstinate. I'm beginning to think she wants to drive me mad."

"It sounds as if being a literary agent is a lot more frustrating than I would have thought," said David.

"No, that's really not the case. I love my job. In particular, I love working with promising new authors that need a helping hand and encouragement to develop their full potential. Catherine Cromwell is that sort of person. For example, she really took to heart my advice as to the six essential ingredients of a successful romance novel."

"Six essential elements? What would those be?"

"While there may be the rare exception, a successful romance novel should have:

* a young, relatively inexperienced girl
* a handsome, mysterious, yet vulnerable man a few years older than the girl
* a sweet, blossoming romance
* a misunderstanding that threatens the romance
* a resolution of the misunderstanding
* a happy ending

Catherine's most recent novel, *A Cotswold Diary*, had all six of those ingredients. In fact, it had the most remarkable resolution of the hero and heroine's misunderstanding that I have ever read. It was brilliant."

"If that's so then why is it so important for you to have a face-to-face meeting with the woman? It sounds as if everything is working out fine."

"David, there is so much more to the publishing business than a terrific story and superb writing. A book has to be *discovered*. Otherwise it just one of the hundreds of thousands of books published each year.

To be discovered, an author should have a platform. Unfortunately, Catherine Cromwell refuses to create a platform or allow me to help her develop one."

"Just what's a *platform*?" asked David.

"A platform is a means by which an author – particularly a relatively unknown author – communicates her presence to others."

"Just how does an author build a platform?" asked David.

"In today's world of book publishing that's usually accomplished by means of social media. That requires a presence on the Internet, and that's accomplished with a Facebook page, a Twitter account, or an author's website. Other ways to signal your presence include speaking at book clubs, connecting with radio and television programs, issuing press releases and writing articles for newspapers and magazines. In short, it's left – mostly at least – to the authors to be their own publicity and marketing department. Catherine Cromwell has expressed no interest, whatsoever, in the development of such a platform. And now, instead of focusing on writing of romance novels, she's gone off into a very different direction – a totally different genre."

"Oh, and what would that be?"

"She started, about a year ago, to write a novel titled *Obsession*. It is, however, most definitely *not* a romance novel. In fact, it is more heart-breaking than heart-warming and, from what she has written so far, there is absolutely no chance that it will have a happy ending."

David was beginning to wish that he had taken the opportunity to read the manuscript for *Obsession*.

"What's it about?"

"The book is yet to be finished but, from what Catherine has written so far, it's about a woman who is obsessed – almost insanely so – with avenging the disgrace of her late husband. It takes place in England, during World War II, and continues to the present time.

"The story begins in 1944, when the woman – her name is Becky – meets a young man who is about to go to war. They marry against the wishes of both sets of parents. Both the young man and the young woman are but 18 years old at the time.

"The man in the story, his name is Jack Timpson, takes part in the D-Day landings in Normandy. He was a member of the Gloucestershire Battalion that landed on Gold Beach that day. Later that year he was wounded and sent to a field hospital. That hospital happened to be in the wrong place at the wrong time. A major battle took place near the hospital. Jack Timpson, still recovering from a head wound, was taken captive by the Germans. He and other Allied soldiers, some Brits, some Canadians, and even a few Polish troops, were sent to a German POW camp."

"Okay, so the Jack Timpson character was captured by the Germans. What happened to him?"

"Becky Timpson, his young wife, was informed – sometime in early 1945 – that he and three other POWs had attempted an escape. Only one of the four managed to make it back to Allied lines. The others were killed.

"The lone survivor, a character in the story named Roy Eaton, received a hero's welcome on his return to England. Two years later he published a book that described his time as a POW and his escape. In that book Roy Eaton portrayed Jack Timpson as a Nazi collaborator and abject coward. Eaton claimed that his fellow escapees, in fact, were forced to subdue Jack so as to prevent him from giving away one of their hiding positions during the escape attempt. Becky was, quite naturally, devastated by what she believed to be outright lies and libel against her dead husband."

"I would imagine so," said David.

"Becky Timpson was outraged by the release of the book and attempted to halt its publication. When that didn't work, she followed Roy Eaton on his book tours and would shout out words such as 'liar," 'cad,' 'scoundrel' – and worse. She was arrested several times for disturbing the peace but that didn't stop her. At least not until there was an attempt on her life. Her flat was firebombed."

"Roy Eaton tried to kill her?"

"Becky was convinced that it was Roy Eaton but there were no witnesses or any evidence tying the attempt to him. Besides that, she required a stay in hospital for treatment of her burns and was in no condition, physically, mentally, or financially, to pursue the matter – at least at that point in time."

"So," asked David, "what happens next in the story?"

"Once Becky was released from hospital, and still fearing for her life, she went into hiding. A few months later she was found eating discarded food from the bins behind a restaurant. She was incoherent, didn't know her name, and was pronounced a danger to both herself and society.

Becky Timpson spent the next 24 years in a mental asylum.

"When she was released, she changed her name, adopting the identity of a baby girl that died years ago. She was hired as a secretary and her performance in that job was exemplary. Becky, however, remained fixated on clearing her late husband's name. Perhaps, even more so, she wanted to kill the man she believed libeled her husband and attempted to kill her."

"How did she intend to obtain her revenge?"

"Becky's appearance had been changed, partially by the passage of time and partially due to the burns she received in the firebombing. She was convinced that Roy Eaton, the man she believed libeled her husband and attempted to kill her, will no longer recognize her and that she could, in fact, walk right up to him and shoot him. That's exactly what she plans to do, whatever the consequences. Becky discovers, however, that Eaton has become extremely wealthy over the years – mostly due to his hero status as the lone survivor of an escape from the German death marches. The man is seldom seen in public and frequently travels between a home in London and his estate in the Cotswolds. Becky decides to move to a Cotswold village not far from the man's manor house believing that will offer her the best opportunity to assassinate Eaton.

"Months pass before she has an opportunity to shoot him. She finds the man sitting in the back of his chauffer driven Rolls Royce, parked behind a store in the Cotswold village. Eaton was evidently waiting for his chauffer to return with something. Becky walks up to the car and takes a pistol from her purse. Roy

Eaton, however, is engaged in reading a document and has his back to her. She stands there, holding the pistol, but cannot pull the trigger. Becky ultimately walks away and Eaton is blissfully unaware of how close he had come to being shot."

"Is that how the manuscript ends?" asked David.

"Not at all. Becky decides to obtain her revenge in another way; to destroy Roy Eaton's reputation – just as he had destroyed her husband's. She is convinced she can find a way to disprove Eaton's story and disgrace him while removing the stain he placed on her late husband's reputation."

"And how does she manage that?"

"The manuscript ends at that point. I really have no idea how Catherine Cromwell plans to conclude the story. Whatever its ending, I find the story terribly sad. The heroine wastes her life seeking revenge. Even if she is able to disgrace the Roy Eaton character in the concluding chapters, it's still a sad, depressing tale."

#####

Dylan Jones took an opportunity to look, once more, out the window of his tiny office, a shabbily furnished office and living space located directly above the only Chemist store on Chambury's high street. The window itself looked out upon the village bakery. Seated at an outside table in front of that bakery was the lovely Mildred Pankhurst ... and David Wallace. Dylan found it hard to contain his anger. Despite his warnings to Miss Pankhurst, she was cheerfully conversing with the damnable Yank – a man who had become a thorn in the side of Dylan Jones.

Things, thought Dylan Jones, were going from bad

to worse. The Yank would not commit to selling the Fleming house and Lord Emsworth and his unpleasant son were losing patience with him. To pile misery upon misery, a Detective Chief Inspector, allegedly famous for his crime solving skills, was now looking into the death of Rebecca Fleming.

#####

Mildred noticed that David had an odd look on his face. "A penny for your thoughts, David Wallace."

"Sorry, I was just wondering what would possess Catherine Cromwell to write such a story. Tell me, what are the time periods in her other stories?"

"Her other stories take place either before or during the Second World War, the period from about the mid thirties through the late forties. Which, now that I think of it, is a bit odd."

"Oh, why is that odd?" asked David.

"Catherine Cromwell is in her mid to late 20s, at least that's what I would guess from her photo. Most romance novelists of that age either write stories that take place in the present time or, in many instances, the 19th century. Come to think of it, she's the only author I represent that writes stories taking place in the thirties or forties."

"Catherine Cromwell is evidently a very unusual woman," said David.

"That she is, unusual and unusually exasperating. I'm beginning to believe that she has a lot of secrets, beyond just that of her address, that she's concealing."

"I would have to agree, and that reminds me that I promised to attempt to explain the gossip and rumors that I'm sure you've heard about me."

"David, you really don't have to explain anything. I

wouldn't be sitting here with you if I was overly concerned about your past."

"Perhaps not, but I still want to address the rumors – some of which, I'm afraid, are actually true."

David proceeded to explain just how and why he had been falsely accused of being responsible for the tragedy at the AXe pumping station. He then admitted that he had taken out his anger and frustration by attempting to drink himself into oblivion. That had all changed, he promised, since his arrival in Chambury.

David then told Mildred the circumstances that had led him to Chambury and the inheritance of his great Aunt's estate. It wasn't until he informed Mildred that he was now "a person of interest" in the investigation of his aunt's death that Mildred's eyebrows were raised.

"From the look on your face," said David, "I'm guessing you hadn't heard about that before."

"No, I certainly had not. But, David, don't you have any witnesses that will vouch for you – people that saw you in Aberdeen during the period of time your aunt was supposedly being overmedicated?"

"Mildred, I stayed in my flat for a month straight – and I had no company. None of the people I had considered to be my friends wanted to be around me. Another problem is that I had at least two blackouts during that month. And, as I mentioned, I was found asleep on the side of an M5 slip road just 70 miles north of Chambury. With that on my record, I can only wonder how I could convince anyone that I hadn't been to Chambury prior to my aunt's death."

Mildred frowned, and then her eyes lit up. "David,

you said that you were drinking yourself silly every night. Just where did you get all that beer and whiskey?"

"I had plenty of whiskey stored away in the cupboard of my flat. But, since the fridge in my flat was broken, I did walk down the street to a little grocery store and buy beer. In fact, by God, I do believe that I visited that store at least once every day."

"David, are you thinking what I'm thinking?" asked Mildred.

"I believe so. That shop likely had at least one security camera. The recordings could prove that I was in Aberdeen during the time period my aunt was slowly being poisoned. It's over a thousand mile drive from Aberdeen to Chambury and back."

"David, you really need to contact that shop owner as soon as possible," said Mildred, checking her wristwatch. "But I do have to run. I have a meeting this afternoon in Cheltenham and I really need to get on the road."

Once Mildred Pankhurst was out of sight, David walked back to the mailbox rental shop. He was taken by surprise when the shopkeeper failed to turn his back on him. Instead, the man stood behind a counter, staring at David but not saying a word.

"Good morning," said David as he walked to his aunt's mailbox. He was stunned by what happened next.

"Good morning," said the shopkeeper.

What the hell is going on, David thought. The man actually greeted me.

David opened the mailbox and found that it contained a single envelope, an envelope that had a Polish return address. He opened the envelope immediately and found that it had three newspaper clippings, all from Polish newspapers. It also had what appeared to be a bill. It was for 400 Euros, in payment – according to the bill – for "news clipping services."

So that, thought David, is how my aunt collected her newspaper clippings.

Chapter 26

Guyton-upon-Cham; Monday, 26 April 2010: Detective Constable Tommi Blake and Police Constable Billy Milne exchanged puzzled glances. They were both waiting, impatiently, for the arrival of DCI Grahame. Keith Grahame had ordered them to be in his office at precisely 10:00 a.m. It wasn't until 10:27, however, that Grahame – without a word of explanation or even a hint of an apology – joined them.

"Milne, you'll go first," Grahame ordered, taking a seat on his swivel chair. "I want a summary of your results so far into the investigation of the death of Rebecca Fleming. Be warned that I do not want a reading from the damn Action Book. I've already read those entries. I want each of you to brief me on what you've found, so far, in your own words. Once your briefings are completed we'll discuss our next steps in the investigation."

Tommi Blake raised her hand.

"Blake, any questions you have can wait until after you and Milne provide your summaries," said Grahame, putting on his tinted glasses. "Until then, Blake, sit there and listen."

Billy Milne's presentation was a bit shaky at first. The young PC was obviously anxious. As his nerves settled, he proceeded to provide what Tommi believed to be a professional-grade summary of his findings. He did not, however, present any facts that Tommi had not known beforehand … until he mentioned David Wallace's drinking habits. Milne had found out that David Wallace rarely left his Aberdeen flat except for once or twice daily walks to a neighborhood grocery and news agency shop. Evidently David's fridge was broken and he would purchase chilled beers from a shop owned by a Pakistani named Abul Hafeez.

Tommi Blake could not contain herself. "Then we need to ask Mr. Hafeez if there are security cameras …'

"Blake," said Grahame, interrupting, "you were told to hold any questions – and that includes comments and suggestions – until after both you and Milne have finished your briefings. Please do not interrupt PC Milne again."

Once Milne finished his briefing, Grahame pointed to Tommi and simply said "Go."

Tommi briefed Grahame and Milne on what she had found out about Rebecca Fleming, focusing on the fact that the woman had taken on the identity of a child that had died in 1926 and, as a consequence, Tommi had – thus far – been unable to trace the woman's life history prior to 1975. She concluded her presentation with a brief mention of Rebecca's seven years of employment as a secretary for a book publishing firm in London and a secretarial stint at a law firm in Cheltenham from 1982 through 1985.

"All right, with what we know now about David Wallace and Rebecca Fleming, what should be the next steps in the investigation? I want your recommendations." said Grahame, looking first at

Tommi and then Billy Milne.

Milne answered first. "Sir, I've already taken a next step. I contacted the Aberdeen City DHQ and asked them to see if the shop owner had installed security cameras and, if so, to send the hard drives the cameras record on to us as soon as possible. I just received, right before this meeting, a confirmation that the hard drives have been put on a train and should be arriving this evening."

"And what about you, Blake?" asked Grahame.

"Sir, I want to determine just what Rebecca Fleming's real name is; I believe that could prove helpful, perhaps even essential, in solving this case. The woman was clearly attempting to hide from someone or something. That someone just might be the person who killed her. I'd like to work with PC Milne on that matter. I believe the two of us should start by examining David Wallace's family tree; we should try to determine the true surname of his great aunt."

"Agreed," said Grahame, "anything else?"

"Sir," said Tommi, "I'd also like to recommend that you and I interview Dylan Jones. I know you believe he had no motive for doing away with Miss Fleming but he certainly had the opportunity to add Diazepam to her sugar bowl. The man spent a great deal of time with her during the week before her death. Furthermore, we really know very little about his background. The only time he was actually interviewed was by the Duty Officer on the day that Miss Fleming's body was found."

"I'll take your recommendation under consideration. In the meantime, continue to pursue the matter of Rebecca Fleming's real name. Milne, follow up on the Aberdeen recordings and assist Blake with the matter of Miss Fleming's name." Grahame then checked his wristwatch. "I have a meeting with the superintendent. This meeting is closed."

Just as Tommi was about to get up, Grahame had a request. "Blake, I hear there's an outstanding Indian restaurant in Chambury. What's your opinion of their food?"

"You must be talking about the Dum Pukht. The food is brilliant … although expensive. I'd recommend the Dumpukht Biryani."

And, thought Tommi, if there is a God then, hopefully, you'll get a nice case of food poisoning. Not enough to kill you, but enough to keep you out of this office for a while.

Tommi Blake felt like screaming. DCI Keith Grahame was, she was convinced, a total ass. The man seemed determined to avoid doing anything by the book and he most certainly had no respect for her abilities. At that moment her thoughts were interrupted by PC Milne.

"Tommi," said Billy Milne, "can we talk? How about the break room?"

Once they had entered the otherwise empty break room, Milne had another request. "Tommi, may I speak strictly off the record?"

Tommi Blake realized that she – and Billy Milne – were treading on dangerous ground. Despite her concerns, she nodded her head in the affirmative.

"Did you happen to notice the book that was lying

on the inspector's desk? Tommi, it was an Agatha Christie novel – one of her stories about Hercule Poirot."

"I saw it, Billy, but what about it? Half the detectives in the force read those. Particularly the old timers."

"I know, but I'm convinced that Grahame may actually believe he's some sort of real life Hercule Poirot – and that the two of us are nothing more than a couple of Captain Hastings."

"So you believe," said Tommi, "that the inspector thinks we're naïve, slow-witted and should be kept in the dark as to what he's thinking?"

"Exactly," said Milne. "Again, speaking strictly off the record, the man doesn't seem to want to reveal his own findings, or even his opinions. For example, consider his reaction to your recommendation to interview Dylan Jones. He avoided a direct answer. Saying that 'he'll take it into consideration' is his way of telling you to bugger off."

"Billy, I don't understand it either.. I just know that, regardless of what we may think of the man, he is the Senior Investigating Officer. We report to him, not the other way around."

"I realize that, Tommi, but the whole structure and direction of this investigation is, don't you think, unusual?"

"I've got to admit that I've never seen a murder investigation conducted in this manner before but, as we were told last year, our HQ is understaffed and underfunded. Perhaps the inspector is attempting to compensate for that, or perhaps he thinks the rules don't apply to him. Whatever the reason, he is still the

SIO on this case."

"Yes, but …'

"Constable Milne, there are no 'buts.' We report to Chief Inspector Grahame … and I don't believe we should say anything more. Consider everything we say from this moment on to be 'on the record.' Now, I've got work to do and I advise you to do the same."

#####

Chambury; Monday, 26 April 2010: After his impromptu meeting with Mildred Pankhurst, David was even more convinced that he was absolutely and desperately in love with the woman. He was determined to do everything he could to have his name removed from the list of "persons of interest" as compiled by the local police. He took that first step by calling the police headquarters in Guyton-upon-Cham and asking to speak to DCI Grahame.

David was told that Chief Inspector Grahame was "unavailable" at the moment and his call was transferred to DC Blake. DC Blake informed David that she was aware of the security camera matter in Aberdeen and that it was already a part of their investigation. She refused to provide any elaboration on that matter or, in fact, any other details.

David decided to spend the remainder of the day reading *Obsession*, the unfinished Catherine Cromwell manuscript. Based upon Mildred Pankhurst's brief summary, he suspected that the story was likely more fact than fiction.

#####

Guyton-upon-Cham; Monday, 26 April 2010: DCI Keith Grahame's rented flat in Guyton contained a bare minimum of furniture: a bed, dresser, armchair, television set, small fridge, kitchen table, and two straight-back chairs. The remainder of his furniture and belongings were in a rental storage unit. They were to remain there, Grahame was determined, until he received a transfer back to his previous post in London.

Downing another shot of vodka, Grahame wondered just how and why he had wound up in a dead-end job in a place full of ignorant country bumpkins. He blamed his predicament on his previous partner, an insolent, backstabbing detective sergeant who relentlessly questioned Grahame's judgment and insisted on different courses of action. It had only been through sheer luck, Grahame was convinced, that the sergeant had solved two high visibility murder cases – and then had the audacity to claim full credit for the arrests while filing a complaint against him.

DC Tommi Blake, thought Grahame, appeared to be doing the same thing, although not as blatantly. Her insistence on pursuing an investigation of Dylan Jones was a waste of time. Besides that, the arrest of a country nobody for the murder of yet another country nobody wouldn't make any headlines … outside of the local country bumpkin press.

An arrest, however, of an American – one who had somehow escaped punishment for his criminal negligence in the death of four men in Scotland – would likely receive national if not international press coverage. Grahame decided, however, to talk with Jones, just in case there was the one in a million chance the man was somehow involved in the death of Rebecca Fleming. He would do that tomorrow.

For tonight, however, he would finish reading – for the fifth time – his favorite Hercule Poirot story, *Murder on the Orient Express*.

Chapter 27

Chambury; Tuesday morning, 27 April 2010: It was a few minutes past midnight when David finally put the manuscript down. He was now absolutely convinced that *Obsession* was most definitely not fiction; instead it was a factual account of his great aunt's 65-year quest to avenge what she was convinced had been the libel and disgrace of her beloved husband – and the attempt to kill her. While the names may have been changed in her manuscript, David's great aunt had been writing a true story – and she, initially under the name of Becky Timpson – was its lead character.

David found it intriguing to find that, in the story, the character of Becky Timpson had changed her name – to Rebecca Fitzgerald – and moved to a small village in the Cotswolds for the purpose of shooting the man who had defamed her husband and attempted to kill her. That village, he was quite sure, was Chambury, and Rebecca Fitzgerald was actually Rebecca Fleming.

There was, however no mention of the lead character having a dog, or of writing romance novels, or – of particular interest to David – of ever having visited Texas. Evidently his aunt did not consider those items essential to the telling of the story. The last chapter of the unfinished manuscript did, however, indicate that the lead character – Becky

Timpson/Rebecca Fitzgerald aka Rebecca Fleming – had found out something of major interest and was about to embark on a trip to Poland.

Suddenly Molly, who had been asleep on the drawing room floor, leapt to all fours and raced to the rear of the house. David, hearing the door handle of the back door being turned – a door that had been locked – picked up a fireplace poker and sprinted after Molly.

The door opened to reveal the figure of Liliana Kowalski. Liliana put her finger to her lips and made a shushing sound, immediately followed by a plaintive request. "Mr. Wallace, please allow me to come in; I'm quite sure I wasn't followed."

David gave the woman a questioning look and then motioned for her to enter. "Come in, Miss Kowalski. But tell me, what are you doing with a key to my house and sneaking around at night?"

"Mr. Wallace, I – like you – am a person of interest in the death of my dear friend, Rebecca Fleming. She is the one who gave me her spare key. Mr. Wallace, I don't want to go to jail and my flat's been secured by the police; that's why I'm asking that you hide me. I also have something very important to tell you, so please let me stay here at least for the rest of the night."

"Miss Kowalski, you are welcome to stay here tonight. But I'm sure that the 'person of interest' matter is a mistake, although I must admit that you didn't do your case much good by running away. Come morning, we should both contact the police and attempt to straighten things out."

"Mr. Wallace, you don't understand. I made the

foolish mistake of giving Tommi Blake a sugar bowl I took from this house. I saw an odd residue on the bottom of the bowl and I asked her to have it analyzed.

"I never, ever thought that I would be the one accused of placing Diazepam in that bowl. I should have never trusted that Tommi Blake; she's a horrible girl and I'm sure she carries a grudge against me."

"Really? What sort of grudge, and why?" asked David.

"It happened about 15 years ago. Tommi was in the library and I caught her tearing several pages out of a magazine. I banned her from the library and reported her to the headmaster of her school. The headmaster disqualified her from sports for a year. I'm quite certain that Tommi Blake has never forgiven me."

David could only wonder if DC Tommi Blake could possibly have held a grudge that long. "I still believe that you need to tell the police that you're back. Running away only makes it seem that you are guilty."

"You may be right, but I don't want to have to deal with Tommi Blake. She'll most likely lock me up and throw away the key. I doubt if that horrid girl will even take the time to hear me out. I need to tell someone – other than her – about what I discovered in Poland."

"You were in Poland? Why Poland?" David asked.

"Do you remember those news clippings you found in Rebecca's house?" Without waiting for a reply, Liliana continued. "In particular, do you remember the most recent clipping; the one from a

Polish newspaper with the photo of a young man and, right next to it, the photo of an old man?"

"I remember," said David. "Both men were wearing rather unusual military style caps."

"Mr. Wallace, those were World War II Polish Army garrison caps. The young man and the old man are not only wearing the same style caps, they are in fact *the very same person*. The photo on the top left of the article was of a man named Piotr Bartkowski, at age 17. The photo on the top right was of Piotr at age 89, and it was taken just three months ago. The article itself is a summary of an interview of Mr. Bartkowski and, Mr. Wallace, it is quite a remarkable interview."

"All right," said David, "so the interview was 'remarkable,' but just why was it of so much interest to my aunt?"

"Let me first tell you about my trip and my visit to the home of Piotr Bartkowski, the man in the photographs. I believe that will explain everything."

"I'm all ears," said David.

"I traveled to Krakow and found the same car hire company that Rebecca had used on her trip. I also managed to find the same driver she had employed – and asked him to drive me to the same destination he took Rebecca to on her visit. He drove me to the town of Mogilany, about 15 kilometers south of Krakow – the same town in which Piotr Barkowski lived.

"Unfortunately, when I arrived in Mogilany I found out that Piotr Bartkowski was dead. The poor man had died, under very suspicious circumstances, just two days after Rebecca's visit. Piotr's grandson is convinced that his grandfather was murdered. Even the police have listed the man's death as a possible homicide.

"Fortunately, for me, the grandson's wife – her name is Katarzyna – had heard everything that had been discussed between Piotr and Rebecca during her visit. The woman was, in fact, in the same room during the discussion.

"Katarzyna was, at first, somewhat reluctant to provide me with the details of that conversation. That changed when I informed her that Rebecca was also dead and that the cause of her death was being investigated. When she heard that she told me everything she could remember about the conversation between Piotr and Rebecca.

"Piotr told Rebecca that he was one of four Polish soldiers attached to a British battalion and that he, himself, was attached to one of its platoons as an interpreter as he could speak fluent German as well as Polish and English. His platoon was involved in some particularly heavy fighting and suffered heavy losses. Piotr and two other members of the platoon were captured by the Germans in January of 1945. The three of them were sent to a Stalag in Germany, near the town of Fallingbostel. They were joined, a week or so later, by another member of that same platoon. The four of them were, in fact, the only surviving members of their platoon.

"Conditions at the Stalag were terrible; little food and not enough clothing to protect oneself from the winter weather. But one of the four men, Piotr called him 'Reggie,' seemed to be suffering far less than everyone else in their hut. In fact, he seemed quite well fed and was able, somehow, to acquire a long, warm winter coat. Piotr and the other two men came to believe that Reggie was collaborating with the Germans. In fact, they were positive that he was a traitor.

"In April of 1945, several months after being taken prisoner, the Germans ordered all prisoners of the Stalag to gather their possessions and prepare for a march. The next morning they were marched out of the camp and to the northeast, away from the advance of Allied forces.

"On the third night of the march, one of Piotr's comrades was able to strangle a sleeping German guard and take his rifle and handgun. That man, along with Piotr and the two other members of his platoon, were able to escape into the woods. Piotr and his comrades, including – unfortunately – the man named 'Reggie,' headed west in an attempt to reach the advancing Allied forces.

"The four men ran into a German patrol and were involved in a brief confrontation. One of their group was killed and another, Piotr, wounded. The three survivors managed to escape and continued to trek west until they reached a hilltop south of the city of Hamburg and along the river Elbe. From there they could see the advancing Allied forces, not more than a few miles away. Piotr thought that they had made it to freedom. Reggie, however, had other plans. Reggie shot both of his companions, checked to make sure that they were dead, and then left their bodies. Piotr was convinced that Reggie did this terrible thing so as to keep them from telling about his collaboration with the enemy.

"Piotr, however, was still alive, although just

barely. Two days later he was found by a farmer. The farmer drove Piotr to the nearest town that had a doctor. Piotr spent the next several weeks recovering from the wounds that Reggie had thought fatal. By then Germany had surrendered and Piotr discovered that he was in what was now Russian territory: East Germany. Piotr spent the next decade in a Russian prison camp before he was able to return to his home in Mogilany, in Russian controlled Poland. It was only just recently that Piotr Bartkowski agreed to tell his story – a brief summary of which appeared in the Polish newspaper clipping."

"I'm guessing that you believe you know who the Reggie character was," said David. "In fact, I'm rather sure that you believe the Reggie in Piotr's story is Lord Reginald Emsworth, the man this village is so proud of."

"That's right; it must be Lord Emsworth. I've read his memoir several times and – other than his lies about how his comrades died – it's very much the same story, with himself as the hero and one of his comrades the villain. Piotr's story is the true story of the fate of the Lost Platoon."

"Miss Kowalski, I agree, and I'm also quite sure that the man Lord Emsworth libeled in his memoir was Rebecca Fleming's husband, a man who died in World War II – at Lord Emsworth's hands – and was then vilified by Emsworth, aka 'Reggie,' in his memoir."

"Rebecca's husband? That can't be; Rebecca was never married."

"Miss Kowalski, I have a manuscript that you need to read. It's written under a pen name but I know that it was my aunt that wrote it. Read it tonight and I'm sure you'll agree."

"I'll do that but, before that, there's one more thing that Katarzyna told me about the visit by Rebecca. According to her, Piotr asked Rebecca to come by the next morning. When she did, he handed Rebecca an envelope and told her to 'make good use of its contents.' Unfortunately Katarzyna wasn't aware of what was in the envelope."

"That's all right," said David, "between what you heard on your visit to Poland and Rebecca's manuscript we should have more than enough to convince the police of the involvement of Reggie Emsworth in the death of my aunt. Tomorrow, we'll go to the police with what we have – and Reggie Emsworth will finally get the punishment he deserves.

"In the meantime, Miss Kowalski, there's an empty guest bedroom upstairs and my aunt's bedroom on this level. Choose whichever you prefer."

"Mr. Wallace, I've never been upstairs in this house; I wouldn't feel comfortable up there. I'll sleep in Rebecca's bedroom."

Chapter 28

Chambury; Wednesday, 28 April 2010: It was a few minutes past eight in the morning when DCI Grahame, DC Blake, and PC Milne arrived at the Fleming house. They were met at the door by David, who showed them into the drawing room where an obviously terrified Liliana Kowalkski was sitting.

Grahame glared at Liliana as he took a seat. "All right, we're here as you asked and we're anxious to hear just what you two are convinced is the solution to the murder of Rebecca Fleming. I do hope, however, that this trip will not prove to be a waste of time."

David first showed the three police officers the piece of fabric that he had found on a Scots Pine tree on the path to the pond where his aunt's body had been found. "It was stuck on a branch of the tree at about shoulder height. Miles Shrewsbury, the man who discovered my aunt's body, told me that she was wearing a nightgown of what I am sure is the very same material. Since the fabric was found at shoulder height it would certainly appear that someone was *carrying* my aunt to the pond."

"Of course," said DCI Grahame, "someone could have just as well placed the fabric on the tree at any time *after* your aunt's body was found. Mr. Wallace, none of the officers at the scene on the morning your aunt's body was discovered saw the piece of fabric on the tree. It's quite possible, in fact, that you, yourself, placed the piece there. Or, alternately, it might have been you, yourself, that carried your aunt's body to the pond."

Billy Milne could hardly contain himself. He had viewed the security camera recordings the previous evening. They showed that David Wallace had visited Abdul Hafeez's shop both the morning and evening of the day before and after Rebecca Fleming's body was found. David Wallace could not possibly have been the person who carried Rebecca Fleming to the pond.

David ignored DCI Grahame's remark. "Miles Shrewsbury also showed me a wall safe that he built for my aunt; the one behind the painting of King George VI," said David pointing to the painting on the wall behind Grahame's chair. "The safe was broken into and emptied. Certainly that must mean something."

"That also wasn't noted by the officers on the scene at the time of the discovery of the body, which means it could have been broken into before or after your aunt's death. It could, in fact, have nothing whatsoever to do with her death. We will, however, check the safe for prints. PC Milne, take note of that and have the safe checked for prints. What else, Mr. Wallace – and what about you, Miss Kowalski?"

"Please, Mr. Wallace," said Liliana, her hands shaking, "please tell them what I told you."

David recounted the story of Liliana's trip to Poland, and the account of the conversation she had with the wife of Piotr Bartkowski's grandson. He then told them what Rebecca had written in an unfinished manuscript, as well as the fact that Piotr Bartkowski had died, under suspicious circumstances, just two days after Rebecca's visit.

David then explained why he and Liliana were sure that the "Reggie" in Piotr Bartkowski's story had to be Lord Reginald Emsworth – and their belief that Lord Emsworth had played a key role in the silencing of both Piotr and Rebecca.

As he spoke he noticed that DCI Grahame's seemingly perpetual look of smug self-assurance had vanished. The man actually appeared to be listening to him.

Tommi Blake exchanged glances with Billy Milne. PC Milne's eyes revealed his feelings; he was spellbound by the story being presented by David Wallace. The notes being taken by both officers were rapidly consuming their notepads.

"Mr. Wallace," said Grahame, "we have taken note of what you have told us. I can assure you that this matter will be thoroughly investigated. Unfortunately, none of what you have informed us of this morning can be confirmed. You must understand that there is no direct evidence of Lord Emsworth's involvement in the death of your aunt – or the death of his fellow soldiers in the war. Everything, although interesting, is either hearsay or unable to be collaborated. There is no way that a manuscript, using fictional names, nor an overheard conversation between two deceased individuals – your aunt and Piotr Bartkowski – is sufficient to implicate Lord Emsworth in either death."

"Perhaps what Liliana and I have discovered is

insufficient in a court of law," said David, "but I would ask you to take these matters seriously. At the very least, consider adding Lord Emsworth to your list of 'persons of interest.'"

"I can assure you, Mr. Wallace, that we will continue to pursue this case until the person or persons responsible for the death of your aunt are found." Grahame then turned to face Liliana. "Miss Kowalski, we have removed our lock on the door of your flat. You are free to go for the moment but I am asking you to provide me with your passport as well as your promise not to leave the county of Gloucestershire until you are informed otherwise."

Liliana reached into her purse and handed DCI Grahame her passport. "Thank you, sir. I give you my word that I will not leave this district until given permission."

DCI Grahame paused as he reached the front door. "Miss Kowalski, Mr. Wallace, I'm asking you to not mention this meeting, nor anything that was said here, to anyone. In particular, no mention should be made of Miss Kowalski's trip to Poland or any suspicions as to who might be involved in the death of either Rebecca Fleming or Piotr Bartkowski. Are we agreed?

David and Liliana both nodded their heads in the affirmative. Both suddenly realized that their very lives might be in danger.

Once DCI Grahame, DC Blake, and PC Milne's car reached the edge of the village, Grahame asked Tommi to pull into a parking lot in front of a garden center. "Blake, Milne, what are your thoughts on what we just heard?"

Tommi Blake was astonished. DCI Grahame was asking for their opinion and it was clear that he meant it. "Sir, Constable Milne and I are nearly finished with our investigation of David Wallace's family tree. We …'

DCI Grahame, grimacing, interrupted. "I asked for your thoughts on the meeting with Wallace and Kowalski. What's Wallace's family tree got to do with this?"

"Sir, please hear me out," said Tommi. "I believe that it could further strengthen the case against Lord Emsworth. What we've determined so far is that the maiden name of David Wallace's great aunt was Rebecca Kealey. Rebecca, or Becky, Kealey was married – at age 18 – to a Mr. Jeffrey Thomas, also 18 years of age. Consequently, Rebecca Kealey's name became Rebecca, or 'Becky,' Thomas in 1944."

"Blake, just where the hell is this going?" asked Grahame.

"Sir, based on what we've determined so far, it's our belief that Becky Thomas changed her name to Rebecca Fleming sometime prior to 1975. We are now attempting to trace Becky Thomas's life from 1945 to the time of her suspected name change to Rebecca Fleming."

"After hearing what we all did this morning," said PC Milne, "I believe that – and I'm guessing DC Blake might agree – we should also trace Jeffrey Thomas's history. What if, for example, Jeffrey Thomas was one of the members of the Lost Platoon – perhaps even one of the members that took part in the escape with 'Reggie?' It certainly looks like that's a possibility."

"Agreed," said Tommi.

"Then I suggest that you two get to it once we get back to the station," said Grahame. "Do not, however, do or say anything that might arouse the suspicions of Lord Emsworth. Lord Emsworth, as I'm sure you both realize, has powerful friends in high places. We need to be circumspect, constables, circumspect."

Both David Wallace and Liliana Kowalski were pleasantly surprised with the outcome of the meeting with the police. It appeared, thought David, that Inspector Grahame had actually given serious consideration to his and Liliana's belief that Lord Emsworth was, at least in some way, responsible for the death of Rebecca Fleming. Liliana Kowalski seemed to be of a similar mind.

"Mr. Wallace," said Liliana, "I believe that our meeting with the police went well even though that horrid Tommi Blake was present. Thank you so much for presenting our case, and thank you again for allowing me to spend the night here."

"That's quite all right," said David. "But, please call me David and, allow me, if you will, to call you Liliana. After what we've been through, I would hope we can drop the formalities."

"You're correct, David, and you may certainly call me Liliana. What I'd like to do now, however, is to return to my flat and, if you'll allow me, to take the manuscript – the one titled *Obsession* – with me. I was so tired that I fell asleep last night before I finished reading it."

"I'd like to first make a copy of the manuscript – in fact I'd like to make several copies. Once I have those copied I'll drop a copy off at your flat. Besides, I'm sure that Molly is itching to take a walk into the village."

Chapter 29

Guyton-upon-Cham; Wednesday, 28 April 2010: It wasn't until after three that afternoon that Tommi Blake and Billy Milne finally completed their investigation into the history of Rebecca Fleming.

"All right," said Tommi, "let's start with her true name at birth. She was born in July of 1926 and her birth name was Rebecca ('Becky') Kealey. Her sister was David Wallace's grandmother."

"Which means," said Billy, "that she was the great aunt of David Wallace."

"Correct," said Tommy. "We also know that Becky Kealey married Jeffrey Thomas in July of 1944 when they were both 18 years of age."

"And," said Billy, "Jeffrey Thomas was a POW in 1945 and ultimately declared dead that same year."

"Yes, and Becky (Kealey) Thomas was arrested in July of 1947 for disturbing the peace at a book signing event in Cheltenham. The author at that event was Reginald Emsworth. A few weeks after that event she was hospitalized for burns suffered in the fire bombing of her flat.

"Then, in 1948, she was declared legally insane and placed in an institution. She wasn't released until 1974."

"That's precisely when Becky Thomas disappeared," said Billy, "and changed her name to

Rebecca Fleming."

"Yes," said Tommi, "she adopted the identity of an infant who had died two days after birth. Then, under the name of Rebecca Fleming, she found employment as a secretary, first in London from 1975 to 1982 and later in Cheltenham, from 1982 to 1985."

"She then purchased her house in Chambury in 1985," said Billy."

"And," said Tommi, "if the story told by Liliana Kowalski is true, then it would certainly appear that Rebecca's husband was killed by Lord Emsworth. There is, however, no evidence – or at least any evidence that would stand up in court under an onslaught by Lord Emsworth's high priced lawyers – to support that supposition. All we really have are the second or third hand words of two dead people."

"Inspector Grahame isn't going to be pleased with these results," said Billy. "He seems to be a stickler for hard evidence – and lots of it. So, Tommi, what do we do next?"

"My recommendation is to contact the Polish police – the ones that investigated the death of Piotr Bartkowski. Perhaps they have some evidence that will connect Lord Emsworth with Bartkowski's death. I also believe we should obtain a copy of the unfinished manuscript that David Wallace referred to – I believe its title was *Obsession*. What I need to do now, however, is attend the interview of Dylan Jones. According to Inspector Grahame, he's agreed to be here at 4 p.m."

#####

The interview of Dylan Jones did not appear to be leading anywhere. DCI Grahame seemed intent on asking one innocuous question after another, questions that Jones easily fielded. Tommi would have loved to ask her own questions but Grahame had ordered her "to listen and learn, listen and learn." Despite the easy questions, Jones did seem to be growing more anxious with each passing minute.

Tommi didn't care much for Dylan Jones. He had moved to Chambury a little more than a year ago. The very first time Tommi had met the man was at the Bashful Badger. He was chatting her up and was about to ask her out when Tommi happened to inform him that she was a police officer. He suddenly remembered that he had an appointment to attend to and excused himself. Two weeks later he asked Tommi's sister to have dinner with him. During that dinner he discovered that Joyce was Tommi's sister. That ended his interest in Joyce.

The interview completed, Grahame had one more question for Dylan Jones. "Mr. Jones, I understand there's a highly rated Indian restaurant in Chambury. What's your opinion of the place?"

"Oh, you mean the Dum Pukht; it's actually just a few doors down from my office. It's quite good. I seriously doubt there's anything comparable in the Cotswolds. I'd suggest you reserve an 8 p.m. sitting. In fact, since I'm driving back to Chambury and since the restaurant is near my office, why don't you just let me make that reservation for you?

Chapter 30

Chambury; Wednesday afternoon, 28 April 2010: During David's afternoon walk into the village to have copies made of the *Obsession* manuscript, he happened to meet Miles Shrewsbury. Miles suggested that it was time for the pruning, reshaping, and fertilizing of the plants and shrubs in both David's front and rear gardens.

"Mr. Shrewsbury, I'm not much of a gardener but, should you have the time, I'll certainly pay you whatever my aunt did for the work. In fact, I'll double that."

"Mr. Wallace, I never charged your aunt and I'll not charge you. I enjoy, more than you can imagine, working in your gardens. Besides," Miles said with a wink, "it gets me out of the house and out of the way of the wife. Lord knows, that's worth something to the both of us. Winston and me will be there in 30 minutes; just let Molly know that her best friend – that would be Winston – will be visiting."

#####

David stood at the backdoor of his house, watching the activity taking place in his very own back garden. Miles Shrewsbury, wearing his gardening clothes – a tweed jacket, wrinkled white shirt, and 50 year-old tie – was whistling "Hail Britannia" while tending to the flowers and shrubs in the garden. Nearby Winston, the cat, and Molly, the dog, were playing what appeared to be their very own rough and tumble version of hide and seek.

"Mr. Shrewsbury, I'm walking into the village. The Wednesday special at the Bashful Badger beckons. I'll leave you to your work and those two," said David, pointing to Molly and Winston, "to their fun and games."

Miles Shrewsbury, pruning shears in hand, gave David a wave. Molly was so involved in her "playtime" that she didn't take notice of David's departure.

The walk into the village gave David time to contemplate his future and, after the meeting that morning with DCI Grahame, he was becoming convinced that he did, indeed, have a future. Liliana's findings in Poland, along with the story woven into the manuscript of *Obsession*, should convince anyone that Lord Emsworth played a role in the death of his aunt – and that he, David Wallace – was innocent.

Having convinced himself that he did have a future, David wondered just how he would spend it. His plan had been to sell his late aunt's house – a house that he was feeling more and more at home in – and fly back to Texas. But that would mean either leaving Molly in England or taking her away from the one and only home the sad-eyed yellow Lab had ever known.

He didn't think Molly would be happy in Texas. After all, she had a "circuit" to walk each morning, a black cat named Winston to play with, and a butcher who gave her dog biscuits.

And there was yet another reason to remain in

England; a woman named Mildred Pankhurst. No, thought David, neither Molly nor I are going anywhere.

Reaching the Bashful Badger, David saw that the Wednesday venison special with Battenberg cake for dessert had attracted quite a crowd. There was, however, at least one empty seat and the man sitting opposite that seat was none other than Dylan Jones.

"Mr. Wallace, back here," said Dylan, waving. "I've saved a seat for you."

David decided that he wanted very much to partake of the Wednesday evening special, regardless of any unwanted dinner companion. "Thank you, Mr. Jones; quite a crowd tonight, don't you think?"

"Oh yes," the venison special always attracts a mob but, to tell the truth, I'm here for the Battenberg cake. Never tasted anything like it; the chef here is a damn magician. By the way, I do think its time that we dropped the formalities; please call me Dylan."

"Certainly, Dylan, and feel free to call me David. But, before we become good chums, there's something I need to tell you."

"And what would that be?"

"I've decided to not sell my aunt's house. I'll be staying here, in Chambury. I plan on making my home here."

Dylan Jones was clearly caught by surprise but, after a moment's pause, he regained his composure. "David, if that's your decision then I promise to never again bring up the subject of selling the house. I wish you the best and, should you ever need any financial advice, do give me a call."

#####

The venison special was excellent but the Battenberg cake was truly fantastic. It was the freshest, most delicious dessert that David could ever recall having, even beating what had always been his favorite, the homemade peach pie of the Texas Hill Country.

"David," said Dylan, "you haven't indulged in the local beer. In celebration of your decision to make Chambury your home I insist that you allow me to buy you a pint of the local brew, a Cotswold Stout."

David had promised himself that he would never again indulge in any alcoholic beverages but he didn't want to insult Dylan Jones. Besides, what harm could it do to drink just one beer?

Chapter 31

Chambury; Wednesday evening, 28 April 2010: Keith Grahame wasn't enjoying his meal at the Dum Pukht restaurant nearly as much as he had hoped. While the food was good, he couldn't stop thinking about the death of Rebecca Fleming. Even more so, he was unable to clear his mind of thoughts of Lord Reginald Emsworth.

Grahame had seen what had happened to those who were brave – or foolish – enough to criticize the rich and powerful. Years ago, Grahame's own mentor, a highly respected Detective Chief Inspector, was on the fast track to bigger and better things until that fateful day he, along with Grahame, had broken up a prostitution ring operating out of an ultra-expensive home in London's Holland Park district. The Madam operating the sexual enterprise, however, just happened to be a distant cousin – evidently a "kissing cousin" – of a member of the Royal family.

Charges against the woman were dropped and, almost immediately thereafter, totally bogus charges were filed against Grahame's mentor. The man was made redundant, his son's admission to Oxford was reversed, his wife left him, and he found himself an outcast and unemployable. Ten months later he placed a revolver in his mouth and blew his brains out. The prostitution ring he and Grahame had broken up was, by then, back in operation and even more popular – and profitable – than before.

Lord Emsworth – like the Holland Park Madam – had friends in high places, friends that could destroy Grahame with a few well chosen words to the right people. Emsworth was considered an "honored friend" of the Guyton-upon-Cham police station. The superintendent's nephew had even attended university with Emsworth's son. Hell, thought Grahame, there's even a damn statue of the man in the center of Chambury.

Even if Lord Emsworth had a hand in the death of Rebecca Fleming, and that seemed more than likely, there was no hard evidence of that. Second and third accounts of conversations between two individuals, now both dead, would be torn to pieces by the big city lawyers that Lord Emsworth would employ.

Keith Grahame's career as a law enforcement officer was already on the shakiest of ground. Even an interview of Lord Emsworth would most likely end his career.

#####

Grahame finished his meal at about half ten, paid his bill, and walked to the parking lot. A light rain had begun to fall, only further dampening his spirits.

As he approached his car he noticed that its passenger side headlamp was broken, with pieces of glass scattered on the ground before it.

"Bastard," said Grahame, "dirty stinking bloody bastard."

Even though the rain was now beginning to come down hard, Grahame made a thorough examination of the rest of the car but found no other damage.

Someone in Chambury, he decided, doesn't like coppers.

He got into his car, turned the ignition key, and headed back to his rented flat in Guyton-upon-Cham by means of the narrow, winding road that connected Chambury and Guyton. As he drove, he continued to struggle with the decision as to whether to initiate a formal investigation of Lord Emsworth or find some way to conclude the entire matter without bringing Emsworth's name into it. This case, he finally decided, is one that needs to join the department's burgeoning list of "cold case files" and be forgotten.

As Grahame approached the sharpest, most dangerous curve on the road, he was suddenly blinded by the bright lights of an approaching car. The driver of the oncoming car sped toward Grahame and, just as he was directly alongside Grahame's car, slammed his car into the side of Grahame's.

Keith Grahame lost control of his car and could only watch in horror as it left the road; tumbling over twice before it came to a sudden stop in the creek bed below. By then the rain was coming down in buckets.

Chapter 32

Chambury; Thursday, early morning, 29 April 2010:
Tommi picked up the phone on its third ring.
Glancing at the clock she saw that it was 1:03 a.m. A
call at one in the morning, thought Tommi, is never
good news.

"DC Blake here."

"Tommi, it's Billy, Billy Milne. Get dressed; we've
got a situation. DCI Grahame was run off the road,
the road from Chambury to Guyton. He's alive, but in
pretty bad shape. He was able to talk; said it was
deliberate."

"Which way was the car heading – the one that ran
him off the road?"

"Toward Chambury," said Milne.

"Any description of the car?"

"No, Grahame just said that the car had its bright
lights on and ran him off the road; said it all happened
so fast that he wasn't able to get a description."

"What about debris?" asked Tommi. "Did they
find any debris from the other car?"

"They tell me that they found a wing mirror and
that there's a streak of white paint on the driver's side
of Grahame's black saloon … hold on a second, I'm
now being told that the color on the back of the wing
mirror is also white. So it was a white car the ran him
off the road."

"Billy, who's there with you?" asked Tommi.

"PC Wainhouse is here. Do you want to talk to him?

"No," said Tommi, "I just want you and Eddie Wainhouse to meet me at the parking lot in front of the Chambury Garden Center. I'll be there as soon as I get dressed."

"Tommi, wait a minute. Did you say to meet at the garden center? That's about 8 miles from where Grahame was run off the road."

"I understand; but I still want you and Wainhouse to meet me at the Chambury Garden Center. Billy, get there just as soon as you can."

#####

Tommi was dressed – in civilian clothes – and in her car within minutes of hanging up the phone. It took but five more minutes to reach the garden center and drive to the tidy little cottage located 50 meters behind the main building.

It was only about a year ago that Hazel Morris, the recently widowed owner of the garden center, had called Tommi to report an early morning break-in at her establishment. As Tommi recalled, two young wasters had broken into the center and stolen several garden tools as well as a nearly new riding lawn mower.

The perpetrators of the crime had been caught within the hour – beginning with the complete prat who was discovered driving the stolen mower back to Guyton. Hazel Morris had, immediately thereafter, installed a state-of-the art surveillance system. As Tommi recalled, it provided coverage of the garden center's parking lot, the road in front of the center, as well as the interior of the main building.

Hazel Morris finally answered the door. "Tommi Blake, what are you doing here at this time of night?"

"Mrs. Morris, there's been a hit-and-run and I need to review your security camera's recordings just as soon as possible."

"They're in the garden center's main building," said Hazel," just follow me."

As Hazel unlocked the door to the garden center, a yellow and blue checkered Ford Fiesta patrol car pulled into the center's parking lot, its blue lights flashing. Police Constables Billy Milne and Eddie Wainhouse exited the car.

"Billy, Eddie, come with Mrs. Morris and me; I need as many eyes as possible."

Billy Milne was the first one to spot DCI Grahame's black Volvo S40. The car, with one headlight out, drove past the garden center at – according to the time stamp on the camera recording – 10:08 p.m.

"That's Grahame's car," said Billy, "you can see his registration plate number. He's heading back to Guyton."

"You can also see how easy it would be for someone waiting on the road to Chambury to recognize the car ... the broken headlamp," said Tommi. "About what time was DCI Grahame's car run off the road?"

"Roughly 10:18 p.m., said Eddie Wainhouse. At least that's the time the clock in Grahame's car stopped."

"Then the car, the white car that ran him off the road, should have returned to Chambury and passed the garden center at about 10:25 p.m.," said Tommi. "Billy move the recording up to, say, 10:20 p.m."

At about 10:28 p.m., according to the recording, a white Vauxhall Astra pulled into the garden center's parking lot, stopping directly under a street lamp. Whoever was driving the car simply parked there for about two minutes, and then drove off in the direction of Chambury's village center.

"That's damn odd," said PC Wainhouse. "It's like the driver wants us to see the plate number."

"I couldn't make out who was in the car but I wrote down the car's registration number," said Tommi. "I'll call it in and we can find out just who owns that white Vauxhall Astra."

A few minutes later Tommi's request was answered. "My God," said Tommi, "that car is registered to a Miss Rebecca Fleming of Chambury."

Tommi Blake, Billy Milne, and Eddie Wainhouse reached the Fleming house at 2:46 a.m. By then the night's rain had turned to a fine mist.

"Eddie," said Tommi, "watch the back of the house. If there's a car parked there, don't go near it – and don't go near the garden shed. Wait until I return."

Billy Milne knocked on the front door of the Fleming house. No one came to the door nor was there any sign of movement in the house. He knocked once more with the same result.

Tommi tried the front door. "The door's unlocked," said Tommi, opening the door. "Mr. Wallace, this is the police. Please show yourself."

This time there was a response, a low growl

coming from the drawing room. Billy Milne turned on the drawing room lights to discover David Wallace, evidently asleep on the drawing room sofa – and Molly, his dog, who had adopted a protective posture.

"Molly," said Tommi, "remember me, old girl? Take it easy, Molly, we're here to help."

"Smells like a bloody brewery in here," said Billy. "Look at all those empty bottles! The man's drank himself unconscious."

Tommi patted Molly on the head and the dog quickly calmed down. "Mr. Wallace," said Tommi, "wake up."

When that failed to rouse the man, Billy Milne attempted to shake him awake. David Wallace's eyes finally opened. "What's going on?" said David. "What are the police doing here?"

"The question is, Mr. Wallace, what have you been doing this evening?" said Billy Milne. "Up to no good, I would reckon."

"Billy, why don't you stay here with Mr. Wallace. I'll be in the back garden."

Tommi left the house through the back door. Eddie Wainhouse was there to meet her. "Eddie, I'm going to check the garden shed. Come with me but be careful not to step on the driveway. If there's any footprints out here we want to save them."

"I already checked for footprints," said Eddie. "The driveway's gravel and, I'm afraid, too hard to leave any footprints."

The door to the shed was partially open. Tommi stepped inside to find a white Vauxhall Astra – an Astra missing its driver's side wing mirror. There was also a streak of black paint, black paint from DCI

Grahame's car, on the driver's side of the Astra.

Tommi put on a pair of gloves and opened the driver's side door. Then, using the light from her torch, she carefully examined the interior of the car.

"See anything?" asked Eddie.

"Nothing, but we will need to check the car for prints. Oh, wait a minute, I do see something."

Tommi picked up a pale yellow blossom that was lying on the floor next to the brake pedal of the Astra. "Eddie, doesn't this blossom look like it comes from that bush, the one to your right?"

"Sure does, what kind of plant is that?"

"I have no idea; let's go in and talk to Mr. Wallace."

David Wallace was now sitting upright on the sofa, looking quite the worse for wear. Molly was laying on the sofa next to him, her head resting on his lap.

"Mr. Wallace," said Tommi, what's the name of that plant, the one with pale yellow flowers near the car shed?"

"Miles Shrewsbury said it was, I believe, an *Illicium Simonsii*. He claimed it was quite rare. Why do you ask?"

"I'll explain later," said Tommi. "First, are the shoes you're wearing right now the same ones that you wore when you drove your car tonight?"

"DC Blake, I didn't drive my car this night nor, in fact, the entire day."

"Eddie," said Tommi, "check the bottoms of his shoes. Billy, search the house for any other shoes and check the soles."

"What are we looking for?" asked Billy.

"Check to see if the shoes are wet and if any blossoms, or parts of blossoms, of the type I'm holding in my hand might be stuck to them. Now, Mr. Wallace, would you tell me how many drinks you've had this night?"

David Wallace's head hurt. On the floor about the sofa were at least five empty beer bottles. But all he could remember was that Dylan Jones had bought him a beer – his first beer in two weeks – and then, try as he might, he couldn't remember anything else.

"I had one beer," said David, attempting to stand, "at the Bashful Badger. Dylan Jones bought it."

"One beer? Then, Mr. Wallace, why are there five empty bottles in here and three more in the kitchen? And why, Mr. Wallace, are you having so much difficulty standing?"

"Tommi," Billy yelled from the stairway, "we've checked the whole house. The man seems to have just two pairs of shoes, plus the pair he's wearing. They're all completely dry."

"What about pale yellow blossoms? Did you see those on his shoes?" asked Tommi.

"No," said Billy and Eddie simultaneously.

"Eddie, would you please take Mr. Wallace to HQ? Billy, you and I need to talk to Dylan Jones. He lives, I believe, in a room in back of his office above the Chemist."

"What about Molly?" asked David. "Someone needs to be with her."

"Who do you suggest, Mr. Wallace?" asked Tommi.

"Liliana Kowalski. Could you have her take care of Molly?"

"I'll call my sister on the way to the station. Joyce can explain the situation to Miss Kowalski."

PC Milne knocked on the door of Dylan Jones's office-*cum*-living quarters. After the third knock the door was opened and Tommi and Billy were met by a pajama-clad Dylan Jones, attempting to stifle a yawn.

"What in the world do you two want?" asked Dylan. "Do you know what time it is?"

"We'd like to come in, Mr. Jones," said Tommi, "we'd like to talk to you about an incident that happened a few hours ago."

"A few hours ago I was asleep; in fact until a minute ago I was enjoying a peaceful night's sleep," said Dylan, "but come in if you want. I've got nothing to hide."

"Mr. Jones," said Tommi, "where were you this evening?"

"I had dinner at the Bashful Badger. I was, in fact, dining with David Wallace. I finished eating at around half seven and then came directly here. I watched the telly until about eleven, and then went to bed. That's it; that sums up another exciting evening in Chambury."

"So," said Tommi, "you were in your flat well before it started raining."

"That's right," said Dylan, "the rain didn't start until, I believe, after eight."

"Mr. Jones, do you mind if we simply look around your flat?"

"Go right ahead. Like I said, I've got nothing to hide."

A few minutes later Billy Milne walked out of

Dylan Jones's bedroom carrying a pair of men's shoes. "DC Blake," said Billy, "the soles are wet and there's a piece of that yellow flower stuck to the heel of the right shoe."

"Mr. Jones," said Tommi, "you are under arrest. Allow me to read you your caution before you say anything. Once that's taken care of we'll be transporting you to the Guyton station."

Tommi could see beads of sweat forming on Dylan Jones's forehead as she stated the caution, carefully reading the words from a card she kept in the inside pocket of her jacket. "Mr. Jones, you do not have to say anything. But it may harm your defense if you do not mention when questioned something which you later rely on in court. Anything that you do say may be given in evidence."

Chapter 33

Guyton-upon-Cham; Thursday, morning, 29 April 2010:
Tommi Blake arrived at HQ shortly after 10 a.m. to
find Police Constables Billy Milne and Eddie
Wainhouse, along with Eleanor White, a Police
Community Support Officer (PCSO), huddled
together in the station's break room.

"Morning, Tommi," said Billy, "how's the
Inspector doing?"

Tommi didn't answer and, instead, looked at the
PCSO and pointed to the door of the break room.
Eleanor White nodded, stood up, and walked out the
door, closing it behind her.

"DCI Grahame is in serious condition," said
Tommi, "although I was told he'll survive. It will be,
however, a long time before he's able to return to the
force. I was asked to contact his relatives but his file
only listed two next of kin, an older brother in York
and a son who's living in Ireland. Neither one seemed
all that upset or expressed any interest in coming to
see him."

"Not surprising," said Billy. "Grahame's not the
type of chap you'd expect to have many friends."

"Enough about Grahame," said Tommi, "what's
the status of David Wallace and Dylan Jones?"

"Mr. Wallace wasn't lying about drinking just one
beer," said Billy. "His alcohol reading was barely

measurable but, at least according to 'Doc' Wilson, he was definitely under the influence. His urine sample tested positive for Rohypnol, the so-called 'date rape' drug. Based on his story about having dinner with Dylan Jones, my guess is that Jones slipped the Rohypnol into Mr. Wallace's drink.

"And" said Billy, "there's another matter of interest. There were no fingerprints, none whatsoever, inside the Astra or on its door handles. There were, however lots of nose and paw prints on the passenger side; but the driver's side of the car was wiped clean. If Mr. Wallace had been the one who ran DCI Grahame off the road there wouldn't have been any need to wipe his own prints from his own car. That's yet another reason, in my opinion, to believe the man is innocent."

"Where's Mr. Wallace now?" asked Tommi.

"He was interviewed and released," said Eddie Wainhouse.

"And Dylan Jones?" asked Tommi.

"Cautioned and interviewed," said Eddie. "His lawyer arrived earlier this morning and ..."

Billy Milne interrupted. "Tommi, it wasn't *his* lawyer; it was one of Lord Emsworth's fancy lawyers. I recognized the man; he was here a few months ago when Emsworth's butler was arrested for public drunkenness. The very same lawyer that got Emsworth's butler off was able to convince our superintendent to release Jones."

Lord Emsworth's Manor House; Thursday, morning, 29 April 2010: "Dammit Jones," said Lord Emsworth, "have you lost your bloody mind? Trying to off a copper; a bloody Detective Chief Inspector at that?"

Dylan Jones didn't answer, choosing instead to stare at his shoes.

"Look me in the eyes, you bloody prat. I want to know why you tried to kill DCI Grahame. And I want to know if it was you that put the drugs in Rebecca Fleming's tea. Speak up, man!"

"Your lordship," said Jones, "I was only trying to do what I thought you wanted. I couldn't convince the pig-headed Fleming woman to change her will as you asked so I added Diazepam powder to her sugar bowl. That did the trick; after that the old fool hardly knew what day it was and I was able to change her will and then have her sign it so that David Wallace was her sole heir – so that there would be no connection to you – and so that you could then buy her house. That's what you asked me to do and I did it, just like you asked. But I swear to God that I didn't kill the old woman, I just drugged her. What choice did I have? You promised me that if I got her to change her will you'd not tell the police about the Guyton situation."

"You were convincing old women to put their money in your investing schemes and stealing them blind," said Henry Emsworth.

"Shut it, Henry," said Lord Emsworth. "Let me do the talking, boy."

Henry Emsworth bit his lip and decided to shut it.

"What about DCI Grahame?" asked Lord Emsworth. "Why in the world did you try to kill him? And, Jones, I want the truth or I'll let Henry finish this conversation."

"DCI Grahame," said Dylan with a shudder,

"interviewed me at the police HQ in Guyton yesterday. He was very clever; asked me a lot of what I was supposed to think were just innocent questions. I could tell, however, that he was on to me ... about me drugging the Fleming woman. If he suspected that then he must have also believed that I carried her to the pond and was responsible for her death. But I didn't do that, damn it; I just drugged her so as to get her to change her will ... just like you asked."

"And you thought you could place the blame for running the DCI off the road on the Yank?" asked Lord Emsworth. "You did a bloody poor job of that."

"Your lordship, it was clear that the Yank wasn't about to sell the Fleming house. In fact, he told me to my face that he had decided to stay here, in Chambury. By running DCI Grahame off the road and putting the blame on the Yank, I thought I could kill two birds with one stone – and then you'd be able to get the Fleming house – and I could get on with my life."

Lord Emsworth shared guarded glances with his son. "All right, but you've made a dog's dinner out of this. Jones, according to my lawyer, sooner or later the police are going to have enough evidence to arrest and convict you for Rebecca Fleming's death as well as running the DCI off the road. That's going to happen no matter how many lawyers I hire."

"But I didn't kill the Fleming woman," said Dylan. "I swear it."

"That may be so, but you will still be blamed for it. Jones, there's only one way to save your skin. That's for you to disappear."

Dylan Jones's eyes went wide. "Disappear? For

God's sake, you want me to disappear?"

"Calm down, man. All I'm saying is that I'll get you a new identity and the means to leave the UK. Jones, I'm offering you a way to save your neck."

Dylan Jones had never been so frightened in his life.

"I'll arrange everything. There's nothing for you to worry about, Jones. Once the paperwork is finished, Henry will drive you to the airport. From there you can fly to anywhere in the world that you choose. I'm offering you a new life, Jones."

Dylan Jones had the feeling that he had a lot to worry about. "Thank you, your lordship. I would, however, like to return to my flat. I need to collect a few things; then I'll be ready to leave."

"All right," said Lord Emsworth. "Henry, once night falls, drive Jones back to the village. Once he collects his 'things,' drive him back here."

"Why can't I just call a taxi," said Dylan, "and why can't I leave now? Why do I have to wait until night?"

"Because, you twit, I don't want anyone to know that you've been here. You'll wait until it's dark and then Henry will drive you to your office, and then back here. By then all the paperwork you'll need to disappear will be ready. In the meantime, it would be best if you stay in the library. If you need anything, just ring Wooster."

#####

Chambury; Thursday, morning, 29 April 2010: David Wallace, with Molly at his side, sat on the oversized armchair in his drawing room. Once his head had cleared, on the drive to the police station in Guyton, it had become blindingly obvious that Dylan Jones had drugged him. David had a faint memory of the man leading him to Dylan's car, parked behind the Bashful Badger. There his memory of the previous night ended.

Thankfully, the police had – after drawing blood and testing his urine and asking a few hundred questions – allowed him to return home, and to Molly. While the police hadn't said as much, David was convinced that they believed he was innocent. He had survived yet another potential disaster with nothing worse than a headache … and the heartache of seeing the damage to the driver's side of the Astra.

"Molly, old girl," said David, "no matter what they do, they're not going to drive us out of this village. This is our home." Molly, hearing her name, looked up at him and then licked his hand.

"Well, Molly, I'm not going to sit here and brood; let's go upstairs. I need to get back to my writing; my 'colpo di fulmine' book beckons."

David was halfway up the stairs when he suddenly changed his mind. "The book can wait. Molly. let's go for a walk."

David stopped at the door of the Chambury Travel Agency. The agency's windows were chock-a-block with travel posters. There were posters featuring the Eiffel Tower, posters picturing the beaches and blue waters of the Côte d'Azur, posters of windmills, and on and on. There weren't, however, any posters – David observed wryly – of any of the sights or landmarks of Texas.

David opened the door and was met with the greeting of a thin, short, balding man of roughly 60 years of age.

"Ah, Mr. Wallace, do come in," said the man. "My name is Clive Birwistle; I've been expecting you."

David was quite sure he had never seen the man before. "You've been expecting me? For what?"

"I assume you'd like to purchase tickets back to America; Texas to be precise. Am I right?"

"No, Mr. Birwistle, you're not right. I have no intention of returning to America, at least not in the immediate future. I simply wanted to inquire about the recent trip taken by my great aunt, Rebecca Fleming."

Clive Birwistle's smile turned into a frown. "Her trip to Poland, I assume."

"That's right, her trip to Poland."

"Don't get much call for flights to Poland around here. Now I've had three people ask me about them."

"Three people?" said David, "which three people?"

"First your aunt, then Henry Emsworth, and now you."

"Henry Emsworth? I assume he's a relative of Lord Emsworth?"

"Henry's his son; his only child. Now, tell me, are you interested in a flight to Poland?"

"Not at the moment," said David. "But tell me, did this Henry Emsworth purchase a ticket to Poland?"

"He did, and he paid a high price for it. He wanted to leave that very day. I told him I could get him a much better price if he'd only wait a few days; but he insisted on flying out of London on that very day."

"Mr. Birwistle, thank you. You've been a big help. I promise that, should I ever fly back to Texas, I'll inquire here first. In fact, should I want to travel anywhere, you, Mr. Birwistle, are the man."

#####

Guyton-upon-Cham; Thursday, late afternoon, 29 April 2010: Billy Milne handed Tommi the phone. "It's David Wallace; he wants to talk to you. Sounds excited."

"Constable Blake," said David, "I believe I have something important to tell you; something that might prove, once and for all, just who killed my aunt."

"And what is that?" asked Tommi.

"I just talked to the owner of the Chambury Travel Agency. He told me that Lord Emsworth's son, Henry, purchased tickets – to Poland – on the very same day that my aunt returned from Poland. He demanded to fly out that very day and, if you recall, Piotr Bartkowski was killed a day or two later. Even if you can't prove that the Emsworths killed my aunt, perhaps it can be proven that Henry Emsworth killed the old soldier in Poland."

"Thank you, Mr. Wallace. We'll definitely look into this … and let me give you my private mobile phone number in the event you have any other information to share. You may call me at this number anytime, day or night."

Tommi gave David her private phone number, thanked him once again, and hung up. Stupid, stupid, stupid, thought Tommi, I should have thought of checking with airline bookings. Instead, I get a call from a civilian. I need to focus; dammit, focus.

Chapter 34

Lord Emsworth's Manor House; Thursday 29 April 2010:
The door to the library had been locked just a few
seconds after Dylan entered. He immediately
examined the room's windows and found that they
too were locked. Dylan Jones realized that, for all
purposes, he was a prisoner in Lord Emsworth's
manor house.

As Dylan looked out a window overlooking several
outbuildings, he noticed that a man was sitting on a
piece of heavy machinery, a John Deere track loader.
The machine's driver was digging what looked like a
foundation for the construction of yet another
outbuilding. Or a grave.

The only sounds that Dylan heard, until night fell,
were those of the track loader doing its work. It was
only then that he heard the key to the library door
turn. The door opened and Henry Emsworth walked
in. He was smiling.

"It's time," said Henry. "Let's go."
#####
Dylan Jones sat nervously in the passenger seat of the
British racing green Range Rover. Next to him was its
driver, the 6 foot 6 inch, 25 stone (350 pounds) hulk
of a man who was, almost certainly, going to try to kill
Dylan.

As Henry Emsworth stopped his car at the end of

the stately home's driveway and prepared to turn right, Dylan hurriedly unlatched his seat belt, opened the car's door, and leapt out. He wasn't sure just where to run to; he only knew that he must get as far away from Henry Emsworth as possible.

As Dylan raced into the woods on the other side of the road, he could hear Henry's footsteps as the fearsome giant raced after him. How in God's name, thought Henry, can a man that big run so damn fast?

Henry Emsworth, running at full speed, bent down and grabbed a piece of wood without breaking stride. The very last thing that Dylan Jones heard, and was to ever hear, was the dreadful sound of his own skull breaking.

Chapter 35

Chambury; Friday, Early Morning, 30 April 2010: David finished writing yet another chapter of the "Thunderbolt" book a little after 1 a.m. Friday morning. Molly, realizing that the typing had stopped, looked up expectantly.

"Well, Molly, it's time for the two of us to hit the sack." With that he turned off the lights in the office and walked to the bedroom. After flossing, brushing his teeth, and changing into his pajamas, David climbed into bed. He was asleep within seconds.

#####

Henry Emsworth, dressed in black and wearing a matching black hoody, turned off the lights of his Range Rover as he approached the Fleming house. He turned the car into the single track road that ran alongside the house and parked in a lay-by. He then put on a pair of gloves and retrieved a house key from his pocket – a copy of the key that fit both the front and back doors of the Fleming house.

Reaching the house, Henry used the key to open its rear door. It was, according to his 80,000 pounds sterling Rotonde de Cartier Astrotourbilon wristwatch, precisely 2 a.m. The lights in the house had been off for about 45 minutes; enough time, Henry thought, for David Wallace to have fallen to sleep.

Henry walked to the stairs leading to the two upstairs bedrooms. He then, ever so slowly, crept up the steps. When he reached the top he found himself in front of one of the guestrooms – the same room in which the lights had been turned off 45 minutes earlier.

Henry crept into the room and picked up a pillow; a move that woke Molly. He then forced the pillow over David Wallace's face – just as he had done when suffocating the old man in Poland. Molly, however, began to bark furiously and seized the big man's right hand in her teeth.

Henry screamed, the high-pitched scream of a man in extreme pain. David took advantage of that moment to push the pillow from his face. He made a fist and struck Henry in the Adam's apple. The big man struggled to catch his breath, his breathing coming in desperate gasps.

Before Henry had time to recover, Molly had sunk her teeth deep into the triceps of his right arm. Henry moved backwards, attempting to shake the dog from his arm. He in fact moved so far backwards that he was standing no more than a few inches from the top of the stairway.

David was desperately afraid that the man would find a way to hurt Molly. He gave Henry a push and watched as the man, with Molly still grasping his arm, fell backwards and down the steps. At no time during the fall did Molly release her grip on Henry's arm.

Henry's head struck the landing with a resounding thud. It was only then that Molly relaxed her hold on the man's arm. David raced down the steps.

"Molly," said David, "are you okay, dear girl?"

Molly stood up, favoring her right front leg. She limped toward David who put his arms around her. "Lay down, Molly, I'll get you some help. Just lay down."

David checked Henry Emsworth's pulse. The man was breathing but he had a deep cut on his forehead. The sleeve on his right arm had been torn off and David could see blood flowing from the wounds Molly had inflicted.

David raced back upstairs and, once he had retrieved his mobile phone, dialed the number that Tommi Blake had given him.

#####

Tommi Blake, accompanied by Billy Milne and two other police constables, found David Wallace standing over Henry Emsworth. Henry's eyes were open but it was clear that he was in a muddled state. David had a fireplace poker in his hand and the determined look on his face made it clear that he was prepared – if not eager – to use it.

"Put the poker down, Mr. Wallace," said Tommi, "we'll take it from here."

David, somewhat reluctantly, put the poker back in its place next to the drawing room fireplace. "I need to take Molly to a vet." said David, "She was hurt while protecting me from that miserable excuse for a human being," David added, pointing to Henry Emsworth.

"I'll have one of our constables take you and Molly to the veterinarian in Guyton just as soon as we sort things out," said Tommi. "First, however, tell us what happened here."

David explained how he had been attacked in his

bed, how Molly had protected him, and how he had provided Henry Emsworth with a wee bit of assistance in falling down the stairway.

"Billy, Margaret, would you please see if you can find out just where Mr. Emsworth parked his car? Mr. Emsworth, just lay there. An ambulance should be here in a few minutes."

#####

Guyton-upon-Cham; Friday, Early Morning, 30 April 2010: Tommi Blake's call to Susan Turner, the veterinarian in Guyton, had roused her from a sound sleep. She was, however, wide awake when David arrived with Molly. The vet determined, to David's relief, that Molly's injury was a strain, rather than a sprain or fracture.

"I'll prescribe an anti-inflammatory that Molly will need to take for a week," said Susan Turner. "In the meantime make sure she rests. When you get home, massage the leg and then apply ice packs. Within a day or so you should be able to take Molly for a short walk but do take it slowly at first. Molly's in superb condition and her injury is relatively minor; she'll be back to normal in no more than a week."

David placed a call to the Guyton police station and, within minutes, a police car pulled up in front of the vet's office. Its driver, PC Billy Milne, drove back to Chambury in virtual silence, refusing to answer the questions posed by David.

"Mr. Wallace, you must realize that I can't discuss this matter. Henry Emsworth is, at this very moment, being interviewed. As soon as certain matters are taken care of, however, I'm confident that DC Blake will provide you with whatever information we are permitted to share."

Chapter 36

Guyton-upon-Cham; Friday, 30 April 2010: Although DCI Keith Grahame was sitting up in his hospital bed, he looked pale. As pale, almost, as the bandage on his forehead. "Are you in pain, sir?" asked Tommi Blake. "Are you sure you're up to hearing all this?"

"Definitely," said Grahame, "Start at the beginning and, in particular, explain just how and why Dylan Jones teamed up with Lord Emsworth and his son. Get on with it woman."

Tommi realized that being run off the road and seriously injured had done nothing whatsoever to improve DCI Grahame's interpersonal skills. She nodded her head and began her briefing.

"Sir, it wasn't Jones's intention to 'team up' with the Emsworths. The man wasn't given any choice. You see, Jones was a con man who preyed on elderly women, mostly widows. Got them to invest in what he claimed was a 'sure thing,' a scheme that would provide them with a generous income for the rest of their lives. It was, however, nothing but a second-rate Ponzi scheme. One of the widows he cheated, however, happened to be a cousin of Lord Emsworth. When Lord Emsworth found out about that he had Henry pick up Jones and drive him to their manor house. According to Henry, they intended to 'give him a hiding he'd never forget.'

"But Jones was also trying, at the very same time, to separate Rebecca Fleming from her money. Jones was able to save his skin by telling the Emsworths that he had overheard a phone conversation, one between Rebecca Fleming and someone in Poland, in which Lord Emsworth's name had come up."

"All right, Blake, don't keep me in suspense. Just what did Jones hear?"

"As I was saying, during the phone conversation Miss Fleming mentioned Lord Emsworth's name, although she referred to him as 'Reggie Emsworth.' She also mentioned several other names, one of which was a 'Jeffery Thomas.' When Lord Emsworth heard that name he went red in the face and ...'

"Who the hell is Jeffery Thomas?" asked Grahame.

"Jeffery Thomas was Rebecca Fleming's husband, a man who died in World War II. Remember sir, from our meeting with Mr. Wallace and Miss Kowalski, that Miss Fleming was convinced, with good reason, that Lord Emsworth, or Reggie Emsworth if you will, libeled her late husband in his memoir. She was also convinced that Reggie Emsworth had firebombed her flat, or at least had someone else do it."

Grahame nodded his head, a movement that brought tears of pain to his eyes. He then motioned for Tommi to continue.

"Anyway, when Jones told Lord Emsworth that Rebecca Fleming was talking to someone in Poland about both him and Jeffery Thomas, Lord Emsworth made a deal with Jones. He ordered Dylan Jones to find out all he could about Miss Fleming and her telephone calls to Poland. Jones was told to continue to ingratiate himself with Miss Fleming and report back to the Emsworths on anything of interest that he learned. He was also told that if he didn't do as ordered he would regret it."

"And Jones was foolish enough to get involved," said Grahame.

"Don't suppose he thought he had any choice," said Tommi as she continued her briefing. "Jones reported back to the Emsworths a week or so later and told them that he hadn't learned much other than the fact that Miss Fleming mentioned to him that she had several hiding places in her house – and that she had told him that someone had done her great harm but she believed she was very close to avenging that wrong. She then told Jones that she was going on a trip and would not be back for several days. She would not, however, tell him where she was going."

"Ah," said Grahme, "that was her trip to Poland, the trip where she visited with … what was his name?"

"His name," said Tommi, "was Piotr Bartkowski, one of the four men – including Jeffrey Thomas and Reggie Emsworth – that escaped a POW march and attempted to reach the Allied lines."

"Ah, so that's how the Emsworths knew that Rebecca Fleming traveled to Poland," said Grahame.

"That's right," said Tommi. "Henry Emsworth went to the Chambury Travel Agency and, after finding out where Miss Fleming had traveled, purchased airline tickets. Henry arrived a day after Miss Fleming left. He admitted to us that, after forcing Piotr Bartkowski to tell him what Miss Fleming wanted, he put a pillow over the old man's face and suffocated him."

"You're telling me," said Grahame, "that Henry Emsworth actually confessed to that killing?"

"To that murder, as well as that of Miss Fleming, Dylan Jones, and of his attempt to kill David Wallace. Henry Emsworth even declined having a lawyer present when he spilled his guts. Sir, we even had a hard time getting the man to shut up. I'm not sure, sir, that Henry Emsworth is right in the head."

"How did David Wallace get involved in all this?" asked Grahame.

"According to Henry, his father ordered Dylan Jones to have Miss Fleming sign a new will; a will in which she'd leave everything to a single person. Lord Emsworth told Jones to find an heir that would be an easy mark; someone – once Miss Fleming died – from whom they could purchase her house. David Wallace fit that bill. Once they had the house they intended to search it from top to bottom – even tearing out walls if they had to – for any documents that Miss Fleming might have hidden that would be harmful to the Emsworths. Once Miss Fleming signed the new will, and under the influence of the Diazepam Dylan Jones added to her tea, Henry Emsworth carried her to the pond behind her house and placed Miss Fleming, still alive, into the pond where she was drowned."

"Bastard," said Grahame.

"Agreed. Oh, there was one other thing that Henry Emsworth told us. When he was carrying Miss Fleming to the pond he told her that she could live if she just told him where she had hidden any documents concerning Lord Emsworth. She told him, and Henry said these were her exact words, 'to go to hell' and that Lord Emsworth should expect a birthday present from her."

"What does that mean?" asked Grahame.

"Henry had no idea but it only made it more important than ever to take over her house. Of course, everything went off course when Mr. Wallace decided not to sell – and when Dylan Jones forced your car off the road. That's when the Emsworths decided to kill both Dylan Jones and David Wallace. While Henry managed to kill Dylan Jones, things didn't go as planned when he attempted to suffocate David Wallace.

"After Mr. Wallace, with the help of his dog, subdued Henry Emsworth and called the police, PC Milne made quite a discovery when he found Henry's Range Rover parked in a lay-by, about 30 meters from the Fleming house. There was a body in the car, the body of Dylan Jones."

"Why," asked Grahame, "did the fool keep a body in his car?"

"Henry – and his father, Lord Emsworth – had decided that both Jones and Wallace needed to disappear ... permanently. The plan was place the bodies of Jones and Wallace in an excavation that had been prepared on the Emsworth estate. The bodies would then be covered by concrete and, so they thought, that would be their final resting place."

"Very good, Blake. Now if you don't mind I've got a press conference scheduled in less than thirty minutes and I suspect you've got things to do too."

#####

Tommi exited the hospital to find a swarm of reporters and television cameras waiting, impatiently, behind a series of rope barriers. Billy Milne was just one of several constables that had been assigned to crowd control.

Tommi shook her head and walked away.

Chapter 37

Cheltenham; Friday Evening, 30 April 2010: After feeding Rupert, Mildred Pankhurst prepared herself a fish pie. Once she sat down at the kitchen table, however, she discovered she wasn't really hungry. Instead, her thoughts were fixated on a man she barely knew – a man who had been accused of responsibility for an accident that had taken several lives, a man who had admittedly "drank himself silly," and a man who was a "person of interest" in the death of his great aunt. Despite all that, Mildred could not stop thinking about him. It was, to say the least, unsettling.

Pushing the untouched pie aside, Mildred decided to watch the evening news. After a brief report on the Queen's visit to Wales the news reader gazed into the camera and said: "How the mighty have fallen; we now take you to Alica McDonald in Chambury, Gloucestershire."

The mention of Chambury got Mildred's attention, as did the report from the village. The reporter was interviewing a sour-looking man who was laying in a hospital bed. The man had a bandage on his head and two black eyes. Standing next to him, smiling broadly, was a older man dressed in the uniform of a police superintendent.

The interview with the man in the hospital bed, a man identified as DCI Keith Grahame, only lasted a few minutes. But those were enough for DCI Grahame to explain how his investigation of the death of a woman named Rebecca Fleming and a man named Dylan Jones had led to the arrest of Lord Reginald Emsworth and his son. The superintendent concluded the interview by praising DCI Grahame for his courage and tenacity, even after an attempt on his life and suffering serious injuries.

Mildred was stunned. While feeling some regret for the death of Dylan Jones, despite his irritating manner, she was ecstatic to learn that David Wallace had been cleared of any involvement in the death of his aunt. She wanted to call him but realized that they had never shared phone numbers. Well, she thought, I know where he – and Molly – live. It's time for a trip to Chambury.

#####

Chambury; Friday Evening, 30 April 2010: Tommi Blake stood up, walked to the television set, and turned it off. "Tommi," said Joyce, "it appears as if DCI Grahame has taken every bit of credit for solving the murder of Miss Fleming."

"The man," said Tommi, "has no shame."

Tommi's mobile phone rang. It was Billy Milne.

"Tommi," said Billy, "did you happen to see DCI Grahame and the 'Supe' on the telly?"

"I saw it, Billy, and I don't want to talk about it. Not now."

#####

Aberdeen, Scotland; Friday Evening, 30 April 2010: Monica Wallace answered her mobile phone. It was Simon Webb, calling to inform her that he would, once again, be working late.

"Monica, baby, don't expect me till at least 2 or 3 a.m. Got no choice; senior management wants a report on our maintenance schedule by no later than Monday. Bye, babe, gotta go."

Monica didn't believe him. She had talked to Simon's ex-wife only last week. She had informed Monica that, during the time Simon had been cheating on her with Monica, he had an extraordinary number of "late nights."

Sometimes, thought Monica, I miss David. She then picked up her phone and dialed the number that Simon's ex-wife had given her.

Chapter 38

Chambury; Saturday, 1 May 2010: Miles Shrewsbury had made it abundantly clear that, while David was free to watch, Miles needed no help in the trimming and pruning of the rear garden. For a minute or so David felt guilty just sitting there on the two-seat garden swing. Then he realized that Miles loved what he was doing. The contented look on the man's face said it all: he was happy.

Molly and Winston were also clearly happy. Although Molly still favored her right leg, her limp was hardly noticeable now. And there was no way to keep Molly inside once she realized that her best friend, Winston the cat, had come to visit.

As David sat on the swing his thoughts turned to the "Texas Giant." David's aunt and uncle, with whom he was then living, had taken David to the 1990 opening of what was simply referred to as "the Giant." At that time the Giant was the world's tallest wooden roller coaster. David was 12 years old and had been looking forward, for weeks, to riding the Giant … until he actually did.

The tallest rise on the coaster was a climb to a height of 143 feet – the height of a fourteen story building. That climb was followed by a terrifying 137 foot free fall. That had been the first and, so he had thought, last time David had ever ridden a roller coaster. Except that, for the past year – and particularly the last two weeks – his life had become a roller coaster ride. He had risen to great heights only to fall to greater depths.

Today, however, he felt that his feet were finally back on the ground. Only one thing marred that pleasant thought; he wanted very much to see Mildred Pankhurst. Unfortunately, it was Saturday and David didn't know where she lived or her phone number. He would have to wait, he realized, until Monday, and then drive to Cheltenham – to the offices of the Passionate Word Literary Agency.

"David," said Miles Shrewsbury, interrupting David's thoughts, "I'm taking a break for lunch. I'll leave you in charge of 'the children," he added, pointing to Molly and Winston. "I should be back in an hour or so."

"Miles," said David, " why don't you just join me for lunch at the Bashful Badger? My treat."

"I'd love to but the wife gets cross when I don't come home for lunch. Besides that, she's fixing my favorite, Bubble and Squeak."

"Say hello to Maggie for me," said David, who had yet to acquire a taste for a meal consisting of leftover vegetables fried in a pan with mashed potatoes.

As David watched Molly and Winston play, he heard a noise behind him. Turning, David was shocked – and delighted – to see Mildred Pankhurst.

"Hello, David. I tried the front door but no one answered. When I heard sounds from the back garden I decided to see if you might be here. My goodness," Mildred said, seeing Molly and Winston, "what are those two up to? And what happened to Molly's leg?"

"Molly had a little accident; I'll tell you the whole story later," said David as he stood up. "As to those two, the black cat is Molly's best friend; his name is Winston. Those two are quite a pair."

"Well," said Mildred, "Molly certainly seems to like cats."

"Molly loves at least one cat, the little black cat that's now hugging her."

"Sweet," said Mildred, "but how about you, David, do you like cats?"

"I've always liked animals in general and ever since I was introduced to Winston, I particularly like cats. Why do you ask?"

"Oh, no reason," said Mildred, "just curious. But David, what I came here to talk about was last night's news report. And, of course, to visit with Molly."

"Mildred, it's wonderful to see you. To tell the truth, I was considering driving into Cheltenham this morning in hope of seeing you. But, since this is a weekend, I decided to babysit those two," said David, pointing to Molly and Winston.

"Why don't we talk over lunch, at the Bashful Badger. Just as soon as my friend, Winston's owner, gets back we can walk into the village and have lunch. That is, if you would care to join me."

"David, I wouldn't have driven here if I didn't want to see you."

Well, thought David, you may change your mind about that once I tell you the truth about Catherine Cromwell.

David decided that the Bashful Badger probably wasn't the best place to have blurted out the truth about Catherine Cromwell, about the brightly patterned package, and the conclusion he had written for *A Cotswold Diary* . Mildred's surprise was now, it appeared, turning to anger.

"Are you telling me, David Wallace, that you knew that your great aunt was the original 'Catherine Cromwell,' and that you finished *A Cotswold Diary* for her? You knew all this and yet you let me search for a person you knew didn't exist? And you lied to me when you told me that you didn't know who Catherine Cromwell was."

"Mildred, I'm truly sorry. I just got caught up in things; I wasn't thinking straight. I …'

Mildred Pankhurst stood up. "I don't want to hear any more excuses. Thank you for lunch. I'm going back to Cheltenham now. I don't think it would be wise for me to see you again."

#####

Tommi Blake, wearing civilian clothes, sat on the drawing room sofa of the Fleming house. David Wallace was seated on the oversize chair across from her. Tommi was saying something but David's mind was elsewhere.

"Mr. Wallace, is anything wrong? Are you feeling unwell?"

"I'm fine, just have a lot on my mind," said David. "Now, what was that you were saying?"

"I said that I'm not here on official business. I simply want to voice an opinion; one that I'm afraid you might find offensive."

"What's that?" said David, wondering just what the bad news was this time.

"It concerns Liliana Kowalski. She's very unhappy

with her position at the library and has been for some time. The council has voted in a number of changes, none of which will be to her liking. Joyce, my sister, is very concerned about Miss Kowalski's mental state."

"Constable, I'm terribly sorry to hear that. But why would you think I would consider that offensive?"

"Because, Mr. Wallace, you may be part of the problem. I'm guessing that your late aunt's will had Miss Kowalski as either the sole or primary heir. It was only because of Dylan Jones that her will was changed ... either under duress or the effects of drugging."

David Wallace was stunned. He sat in silence for a minute before answering. "Constable, you're absolutely right. I've been so focused on clearing my name, and dealing with several personal matters, that I simply didn't think about my aunt's real intentions. You can be assured, however, that I will correct that oversight as soon as possible. This house and everything in it is rightfully the property of Miss Kowalski."

"Mr. Wallace, since I'm not here in an official capacity – and since we are neighbors - may I call you David? And please, do call me Tommi."

David nodded his head in the affirmative.

"David, while I'm sure this is a terrible shock, I believe it is the right thing to do. I'm quite sure that's what your aunt wanted."

David simply nodded. It seems, thought David, that my roller coaster ride hasn't ended.

#####

Liliana Kowalski's flat was chock-a-block with bookshelves and books. David wondered if she even had a bed, or if the woman simply slept on the floor next to her beloved books.

"So, David, just what was so important that you needed to see me right away? Good news, I hope."

"Yes, Liliana, I believe you will like this news. Liliana, since my great aunt's will was bogus, and since I doubt very much that she intended to leave everything – or even anything – to me, I'm here to tell you that – on Monday – I intend to transfer the estate, including all monies, to you. Liliana, you're going to have a new home for you and your books."

"David," said Liliana after recovering from her shock, "that's very kind of you but I do not want, and never did want, Rebecca's house. My plan – at least when I thought I was to be the heir to her estate – was to sell it, its furnishings, and her car as soon as possible. I'd then use the proceeds to help me start a new life, one in which I could be the master of my own destiny."

"Well, come Monday, you can do just that."

"How much money did you inherit, David?"

"After estate taxes and fees, the account has about 240,000 pounds in it. That's all yours now."

"I don't want the house, its furnishings, or the car. And, considering how well you and Molly have bonded, I want her to stay with you. What I would like, however, is 200,000 pounds. That's precisely what I need to start a new career.

"David, even if I survive the forthcoming changes at the library, I would be miserable there. What I want to do is to establish a business, a business that will allow me to spend as much time as I please with my first love: books. I've even looked into the purchase of an empty store in Guyton. It's perfect for what I've planned. I'll sell books in its front room, restore books in the back room, and live in the upstairs quarters.

"So, David, may we settle this matter? You provide me with 200,000 pounds … and your best wishes for my success and then you and Molly make your home in Chambury."

"That's very generous of you, Liliana. I accept … and you certainly have my best wishes, and my promise to provide you with whatever other financial assistance you might need in the future, assuming I'm able to establish a new career here in Chambury."

"What, David, might that new career be?"

"I want to write; I want to write novels. In fact, I hope to write books that would be worthy of display in your bookstore."

Liliana extended her hand. "Let's shake on that, and here's to our new lives."

David shook her hand. "Liliana, do you see the irony in this?"

"What do you mean?"

"You said that if you had inherited my aunt's estate you would have immediately sold everything. Had Reggie Emsworth realized that, there would have been no need to go to the trouble of changing my aunt's will. He could have just purchased the house from you."

Chapter 39

Aberdeen, Scotland; Saturday, 1 May 2010: Monica Wallace examined the thirteen photographs that the detective she hired had given her. The man in each photo was definitely Simon Webb, the man she had been living with for nearly a year – the man who had promised to marry her once his divorce was finalized. There were, Monica noticed, three different women in the pictures, often in a state of undress.

Monica winced. She had suspected that Simon may have been cheating on her but this was too much. Two of the women in the photographs were her friends. The other was her maid.

Why, she wondered, had she divorced David to become entangled with such a cheating, lying low-life? Then again, she realized, she had done very much the same thing to David.

Simon called to tell her that he would be "late" once again. "Lots of work" to do at the office. That suited Monica just fine; she too had "lots of work" to do at home.

The key to Simon's roll-top desk was, she recalled, on a bookshelf behind Simon's desk. It had been only by chance that she had walked past Simon's home office and saw him hiding the key. Monica struggled to remember which book he had hid it behind. First she pulled out *The One Minute Manager*. That title, she thought, pretty much described Simon Webb. No key. Then she replaced the book and pulled out one titled *The 7 Habits of Highly Effective People*. The key was there.

Monica inserted the key in the lock to the roll-top desk. Opening it, she found Simon's personal computer, a computer that he had warned her to never touch. "Don't, dear," he had said, "ever touch that computer. It contains nothing of interest to you, but it's where I store a copy of my company correspondence. Lots of dull reading, but it must be saved. No choice."

After three hours of searching, Monica finally found the mail folder she was looking for. She forwarded a copy of the folder and its contents to her own computer as well as that of her lawyer, Nigel Brimbel. She then turned off Simon's computer, closed the desk, locked it, and returned the key to its hiding place.

Cheltenham; Saturday, 1 May 2010: Mildred, upon returning to her flat, was greeted with a swat on her ankle by Rupert. Once the cat had made his displeasure with her absence clear, he begged to be picked up and held.

"Rupert, you are a strange little creature. Perhaps you need a companion to keep you occupied while I'm out. Perhaps a sad-eyed yellow Lab."

No, she thought, I don't want to see David Wallace again. I just want to focus on my work and, ever since I met that man, I've not given it the attention it deserves.

Chapter 40

Chambury; Friday, 14 May 2010: David, exhausted by his several weeks-long effort, finally finished – with the exception of a concluding chapter – the draft of the novel he had decided to title *The Thunderbolt*. He placed the manuscript in a large manila envelope. He had poured his heart and soul into the novel and now, David was convinced, it was time to send it to the Passionate Word Literary Agency in care of Miss Mildred Pankhurst.

"Molly, let's take a walk."

Molly, who had been amusing herself with a crumpled sheet of paper, turned and raced down the stairs. Seconds later she returned and laid her walking collar and leash at David's feet.

#####

David strolled into the mailbox rental shop, carrying the manuscript for *The Thunderbolt*, and walked toward the row of mailboxes. The shopkeeper, standing behind the shop's counter, stared straight at David.

"Good afternoon, Mr. Wallace, we need to talk."

David, nonplussed by the unexpected greeting, walked to the counter. "Yes, what would you like to talk about?"

"Two things," said the shopkeeper. "First, if you wish to retain your late aunt's mailbox, the rental fee for the next three months must be paid."

"No problem," said David. "How much do I owe you?"

"One hundred and ten pounds."

David reached into his wallet and counted out 110 pounds. "You said there were two things you wanted to talk about. What might the other be?

"The postal service just provided me with an Express letter for you. The person who sent it simply addressed it to Mr. David Wallace of Chambury, Gloucestershire. Haven't had time to place it in your mailbox," the shopkeeper added, handing David the envelope.

"Thank you," said David. Examining the return address on the envelope, David saw that is was from "Nigel Brimbel, Solicitor," of Aberdeen, Scotland. Dammit, thought David, this is from Monica's lawyer. What could she want now?

David opened the envelope to find a brief letter and a newspaper clipping from the *Aberdeen Press and Journal*. The letter was indeed from Monica's lawyer, the man who had represented her in their divorce proceedings. It was not, however, about the divorce. Instead it was about Simon Webb, David's former boss at AXe – the man whose lies had cost David his job and reputation.

> Dear Mr. Wallace:
>
> Enclosed is a newspaper clipping that I believe you will find interesting. Allow me to provide some background and supply a few details that were omitted in the

article.

Monica, your ex-wife, discovered a file on Simon Webb's personal home computer that stored his emails while employed at the AXe corporation. These are emails that Simon Webb, and the firm, had previously claimed were lost.

Several of the emails are those transmitted between you and Mr. Webb with regard to the defective seals on some of the firm's pumps that you (repeatedly) warned about.

Those emails, plus a confession by Simon Webb and another (former) AXe employee serve to completely exonerate you. AXe management has now admitted complicity in this miscarriage of justice. Based on my sources, it would seem certain that they will offer you your job back plus remuneration in the amount of twice what had

```
been  your  yearly  salary
at AXe.
   I  advise  you  not  to
agree  to  their  proposed
settlement. Based  on  the
harm  you  have  suffered, I
am  quite  positive  that
you  should - and  can -
receive  far  more  in
compensation. Should  you
be  interested, I  can
provide  you  with  a  list
of  highly  qualified
lawyers  that  would  be
delighted  to  handle  your
case.
         Sincerely,
 Nigel Brimbel, Solicitor
          #####
```

David read the note twice, hardly believing his eyes. So, he thought, I'm no longer a "person of interest" in my aunt's death. I'm no longer being blamed for the pumping station tragedy. I'm no longer a penniless drunk. But, unfortunately, the woman I love no longer wants to see me.

"Sir," said David to the shopkeeper, "I'd like have a copy of this letter and newspaper article made, and then I want to place them in this manila envelope and have it mailed to the person on the address."

Chapter 41

Cheltenham; Monday, 17 May 2010: Fiona Branch, the owner of The Passionate Word Literary Agency, had been watching Mildred Pankhurst with growing concern. Mildred, normally eager to engage in conversation with the other agents, had gone almost silent. The once bright, cheerful woman had been brooding for at least two weeks.

"Mildred," said Fiona, "there are lots of other fish in the sea. For goodness sake, you've never even been on a date and you've never even kissed the man. My advice is to forget this David Wallace person. The best way to do that is to find someone else; someone who deserves a woman like you."

"I have forgotten the man," said Mildred, wishing that were true. "He means nothing to me."

"Then why are you so glum?

Mildred didn't want the conversation to continue. She came up with an answer she thought might satisfy Fiona. "The reason I'm 'glum' is because of Rupert. He's not been feeling well and I'm concerned. As far as David Wallace goes, I rarely if ever think about the man."

Before she got the last words out of her mouth, Mildred suddenly realized that she was doing exactly the same thing to Fiona that David had done to her. She had lied.

The package arrived at the offices of The Passionate Word Literary Agency at 2 p.m. Mildred examined the return address on the manila envelope. It was from Catherine Cromwell.

Mildred considered throwing the package into the trash but her curiosity got the best of her. She opened the package to find a manuscript titled *The Thunderbolt*.

It was a few minutes before midnight and Rupert was growing increasingly impatient. "Settle down, Rupert," said Mildred. "I've only got a few more pages to read. Then we can both go to bed."

Turning the next page of *The Thunderbolt*, Mildred was surprised to see a note, rather than the first page of the conclusion to the novel:

Dear Mildred:

I don't blame you for being angry with me. I realize now that I should have told you the truth about Catherine Cromwell. I'm not even sure myself as to why I didn't want to reveal her identity, or of my part in finishing the novel, *A Cotswold Diary*. All that I can say is that I am desperately sorry and I cannot stop thinking about you.

You told me that there

```
are     six     essential
ingredients    in     a
successful romance novel.
As I recall, the last two
were: a resolution of a
misunderstanding and   a
happy ending.
   Mildred, I desperately
want The Thunderbolt to
have a happy ending.
-- David
```

Mildred turned that page over and found Xeroxed copies of a letter from a lawyer named Nigel Brimbel and an article from an Aberdeen newspaper.

"Well, Rupert, just how do we deal with this?"

Chapter 42

Chambury's Pedestrian Zone; Saturday, 22 May 2010: "The 22nd of May," said Joyce Blake, "is the 90th birthday of Lord Emsworth, or I should say, Reggie Emsworth. Now that he's been found out for what a miserable man he really is, the committee decided that we'd change what was to be his birthday celebration into something much more meaningful. From now on, every 22nd of May in Chambury will be dedicated to the men of the Lost Platoon and, in particular, to Jeffrey Thomas, your great aunt's husband."

"That's great," said David, "I only wish she could have lived to see this."

"Yes," said Liliana, "but I must say that I feel her presence. Perhaps she is watching."

David shifted his attention from the marchers to the front of the Mailbox rental shop. Its gruff owner was handing out flyers – lots of flyers – to several village youngsters. What, thought David, is that man up to?

"There's Tommi," said Joyce, "doesn't she look grand? And just look at how many members of the Guyton police headquarters are in the parade."

David wasn't listening. Instead, he was watching a dozen or so young boys hand out flyers. Finally, one approached him.

"Mister," said the boy, "I've been told to tell

everyone that this is Rebecca Fleming's birthday gift to Lord Emsworth."

David looked at the flyer. It was a Xeroxed statement, signed by Piotr Bartkowski.

"My God," said Liliana. "This really is a 'birthday present' from Rebecca. It details everything that Piotr Bartkowski told her about the fate of four members of the Lost Platoon. Too bad Reggie Emsworth and his son aren't here to see this."

David watched as the mailbox rental shop owner stood in front of his store, his arms crossed over his chest and – perhaps for the first time ever – smiled.

#####

As the final members of the parade marched past, David saw a familiar face on the opposite side of the pedestrian zone. It was a beautiful young woman. She was waving. She was smiling. It was Mildred Pankhurst.

Cast of Characters

LEADING ROLES:

David Wallace: Born and raised in Texas, disgraced and divorced in Scotland, and sole heir to the estate of Rebecca Fleming.

Dylan Jones: The executor of the will of Rebecca Fleming.

DC Thomasina ("Tommi") Blake: Detective Constable Tommi Blake: a resident of Chambury and assigned to the Guyton-upon-Cham police station.

DCI Keith Grahame: Detective Chief Inspector Grahame: a recent transfer to the Guyton-upon-Cham police headquarters.

Mildred Pankhurst: Literary agent at The Passionate Word Literary Agency, Cheltenham.

Rebecca Fleming: Deceased resident of Chambury and allegedly the great aunt of David Wallace.

Catherine Cromwell: Reclusive romance novelist and client of Mildred Pankhurst.

Liliana Kowalski: Head librarian, Chambury. Rebecca Fleming's closest friend.

Lord Reginald Emsworth: World War II hero and owner of stately home some 10 miles from Chambury.

Henry Emsworth: The son of Lord Emsworth. A collector of expensive watches and automobiles.

PC Billy Milne: Police Constable assigned to the Guyton-upon-Cham police headquarters

SUPPORTING CAST:

Joyce Blake: Sister of Tommi Blake and assistant librarian in Chambury

Simon Webb: Former boss of David Wallace at the AXe Corporation.

Monica Wallace: Ex-wife of David Wallace and lover of Simon Webb.

Frank Owen: Butcher shop owner, Chambury.

Mailbox rental shop owner: Gruff, unfriendly owner of the Chambury mailbox rental shop.

Wooster: Lord Reginald Emsworth's butler.

Andrew Dombey: Senior partner, Dorrit and Dombey Financial Services, Cheltenham.

Edward Tulkinghorn: Solicitor, Dorrit and Domney.

Miles Shrewsbury: Neighbor of Rebecca Fleming and the man who discovered her body.

Maggie Shrewsbury: Wife of Miles Shrewsbury and avid reader of *The Guardian*.

Piotr Barkowski: Polish soldier attached to the "Lost Platoon."

Katarzyna Bartkowski: Wife of the Grandson of Piotr Barkowski.

Nigel Brimbel: Monica Wallace's lawyer

ANIMALS: [NOTE – No animals were harmed in the writing of this book]

Molly: Yellow Labrador Retriever (*the* Dog at the Gate)

Winston: Black cat (owned by Miles Shrewsbury)

Rupert: A cat (owned by Mildred Pankhurst)

ABOUT THE AUTHOR

James Ignizio

James Ignizio has worked as a farm hand, surveyor, professor, and (an actual) rocket scientist. An ardent Anglophile, his favorite authors include Orwell, Kipling, Milne, Dickens, and Agatha Christie. His interests range from orbital mechanics and artificial intelligence to rugby and American football. James is a survivor ... of polio, rheumatic fever, a near fatal car accident, Midwestern winters, and Texas summers. He and his wife live and write in the Hill Country of Texas.

PREVIEW

BENT SPUR PRESS
PROUDLY PRESENTS

THE LAST ENGLISH VILLAGE

A novel by
James Ignizio

http://bentspurtx.wix.com/jamesignizio

Turn the page for a preview of
The Last English Village …

PREVIEW

1
22 DECEMBER 1943:
LOWER FRITHTHINGDEN, ENGLAND

Reginald "Reg" Johnson, Warrant Officer Class 2 of the 43rd Wessex Light Infantry Regiment, stood silent vigil outside one of the matching coal-black Rolls-Royce Phantom IIIs. The choir, housed in the village church some hundred yards away, could be clearly heard. They were singing "Away in the Manger" and doing, in Reg's opinion, a damn fine job of it.

The left rear window of the other Phantom III, the one with "the man" in it, was open. Cigar smoke drifted from the window and floated lazily upward, disappearing into the afternoon sky.

While Reg enjoyed the singing, he was baffled as to just why they had paused here on their journey back to London. The village was several miles off the main road; yet they had driven at top speed to get here, only to sit and listen to a children's choir.

Reg's eyes caught those of Captain Enfield. Enfield shrugged his narrow shoulders. He too had no idea as to the reason for the unusual stopover.

It was then that Reg thought he heard the distant sound of one or more aeroplanes. If he was not mistaken, the all too familiar hum to the northeast was that of a German bomber, a twin-engine Ju88. However, the sound was rapidly diminishing. The aeroplane was evidently heading east, away from the English coastline, so he said nothing.

A moment later Reg's keen hearing picked up the sound of yet another aeroplane; this one headed in the general direction of the village. It was a four-engine craft, from the sound of it one of the Yank's big B17s, a "Flying Fortress."

Just as the choir began the first chorus of "Hark the Herald Angels Sing," Reg happened to look skyward. The thick cloud cover that had enveloped the countryside that day had broken and a beam of brilliant sunlight illuminated the nearby church. But Reg's interest was drawn to an object, drifting slowly downward from the sky.

"Sir, look there," said Reg, pointing skyward. "That looks like a parachute. What do you make of it?"

"Bloody hell," exclaimed Captain Enfield, "that parachute is connected to a German mine. God help us; I do believe it's headed for the church."

Reg and the Captain simultaneously yelled out warnings to the occupants of the Phantom IIIs. By then the parachute bomb was floating no more than five hundred feet above the church. By then it was – to all appearances – too late to do anything.

Although twelve-year-old Tommy Hawkes's headache

and fever had finally started to fade, his boredom grew worse by the minute. With nothing else to do and nowhere else to go, he continued what he had been doing for at least two hours: counting the birds that covered the wallpaper of his bedroom.

While tallying the number of bluebirds on the border, he was distracted by the clanking noises of the dishes his mother was washing. She tunelessly hummed "Silent Night," over and over again … and it was driving him mad! It was bad enough to be sick, bad enough to miss the Christmas play, but now he had to endure his mother's off-key humming. Although he dearly loved his mum, her inability to carry a tune was legendary in and around Lower Friththingden.

Without warning, Tommy's bed – along with the two-hundred-year-old solid brick farmhouse – shook violently. Two windowpanes in his room cracked and a third splintered, scattering shards of glass across the wooden floor. Almost simultaneously, the sound of an enormous explosion, coming from the direction of the village, shattered the quiet of the winter afternoon.

Downstairs Tommy's mother let out a shriek, which was followed by the unmistakable sound of dishes breaking. Shaking with fright, Tommy raised himself to a sitting position. As he looked out his bedroom window, a dark shadow sailed directly over the house. The young boy watched in a mix of horror and fascination as a large aeroplane pancaked to an abrupt landing in the pasture behind the house.

Although he was certain it would explode, the only upshot of the landing was a huge cloud of dust – followed by the sounds of the craft breaking in half. At first Tommy thought it must be a downed German bomber, but, as the dust settled, he was able to make out the markings on the broken fuselage. It was an American aircraft, one of their B17s, the famous Flying Fortress he had read so much about.

"Tommy," his mother cried from downstairs, "don't you dare move from that bed! I'll take care of matters." With that, he heard the kitchen door swing open and, a second later, slam shut.

Returning his gaze to the battered aircraft, Tommy watched as five men slowly emerged from the wreckage. Four of them looked dazed but none the worse for wear. The fifth, the tallest of the group, had a white bandage wrapped about his skull, almost completely covering the bloodied left side of his head.

The injured man stumbled and almost fell, dropping something from his right hand. He immediately went to his knees, frantically pawing the grass around him, trying to find whatever it was he had dropped. Two of the other crewmembers grabbed him by his arms and pulled him, protesting, to his feet.

Tommy studied the downed bomber, wondering where the rest of the crew were. He was almost certain that a B17 carried a crew of ten. But there was no movement from within the aeroplane, and none of the survivors seemed inclined to return to the wreckage. There were, he guessed, either five bodies in the fuselage or else the other crewmembers had bailed out. He prayed for the latter.

Tommy watched as his mother ran toward the men. Using every bit of energy he had, he swung his legs over the edge of the bed and reached for his prized Kodak Six-20 Folding Brownie camera on the bookcase. He was, by God, determined to get a picture of this momentous event.

The sudden movement, however, nauseated him and

he had to struggle to keep from throwing up. By the time he had seized the camera and returned to the window, nothing was to be seen but the aeroplane. He heard the kitchen door open and the sounds of boots against the tile floor below.

Disappointed but undeterred, Tommy aimed the camera and took three quick snapshots of the broken aeroplane. He was ready to take a fourth when he heard yet another disconcerting sound. Two large motorcars, a matched pair of sleek black Rolls-Royce Phantom IIIs, roared into the garden behind the house – driving right through the recently painted picket fence. The car doors swung open and men streamed out of the vehicles. One group approached the plane; another headed toward the house. Most of the men were in military uniform but at least two were civilians, well dressed and important looking. Even though the civilians had their backs to him, Tommy thought that there was something very familiar about the shorter, stocky man.

Tommy raised his camera once again and took two more pictures. Exhausted by the effort, he returned the camera to its place on the bookcase and lay back down on the bed, breathing heavily – his head pounding. Downstairs he could hear the excited, muffled voices of several men speaking at once. Seconds later he fell into a troubled sleep, dreaming of aeroplanes and bluebirds falling from the sky.

2
23 DECEMBER 1943:
LOWER FRITHTHINGDEN, ENGLAND

"Tommy, are you awake?" Tommy stirred, opened his eyes and saw his mother standing over him. The light from the late morning sun filled the small room.

"Yes, Mum," he answered, wondering what her reaction would have been if he had said no.

"How are you feeling, luv? You've slept for near on fifteen hours straight."

"Better, Mum, much better."

"That's wonderful, I thought that nasty cold would pass soon," Tommy's mother replied, and then abruptly changed the subject. "Well, Tommy, my dear boy, we had quite the exciting afternoon and evening yesterday. Have you had a chance to look out your window?"

Suddenly Tommy remembered everything, the explosion in the village, the aeroplane falling from the sky, the swarm of men leaping from the two grand motorcars and, most of all, the tall Yank with the bandaged head.

"Mum," said Tommy, raising himself to a sitting position and pointing out the window, "I saw that aeroplane crash. But before that there was a huge explosion, and right after that the aeroplane crashed into our pasture."

Excited, Tommy's words came faster. "Mum, I saw five Yanks climb out of the wreckage; then two splendid Rolls-Royces drove right into our garden. Phantom IIIs, Mum, can you believe that? Look, you can see where they ran straight through the fence!"

A worried look came over his mother's face and she placed a reassuring hand on the boy's shoulder. "Tommy, you must have been delirious. An aeroplane certainly did crash into the pasture, as you can plainly see. But it was a German craft, and no one on it survived. The explosion you heard a moment before the crash was a German parachute mine scoring a direct hit on the *Sow and Centipede* pub – which was, praise God, empty at the time. The men in that aeroplane must have dropped that horrid device."

Pausing briefly, Tommy's mother continued, her face taking on an uncharacteristically grim and determined look. "There were no Rolls-Royces either, luv, just two military lorries – and they came to inspect the wreckage and remove the bodies."

Tommy could hardly believe his ears. Had he really been delirious? He looked out the window once more, focusing intently on the wreckage of the aeroplane. There was something wrong. The markings on the fuselage had been removed – or, more likely, painted over. There were, in fact, no markings to be seen, either Yank or Jerry. But Tommy had seen enough pictures of B17s to know that what remained in the pasture was indeed a Flying

Fortress. He turned to his mother, about to reply. She, in turn, put her finger to her mouth and shushed him.

"Tommy, listen carefully to me. You did *not* see any men climb out of that wreckage. Everyone on board died in that crash. There were two military transports in the garden, and, as I said, they came and carried the bodies away. There will be a crew coming this afternoon to remove the wreckage. So you make sure to stay inside. Do you understand, son? Inside!"

Tommy swallowed hard. He found it difficult to believe his ears. Never in his life had he known his mother to tell a lie. "But Mum, I swear I saw the five Yanks – and the two grand motorcars. I swear it."

"No, child, for the last time you did *not* see any such thing. You imagined all that. Do you understand? This is very important, Tommy. You most certainly did not see any Americans, and you must *never* tell anyone that you did. *Never.* Do you understand?"

Tommy wanted to protest but thought better of it. Clearly, either he had actually been delirious or else his mother thought it extraordinarily important that he hadn't seen five live Americans. "I understand, Mum," he replied, not understanding at all.

After dressing, Tommy trod, a bit unsteadily, down the stair steps and into the kitchen. There he had his usual breakfast of tea, Weetabix, and fresh cream. Waiting until his mother was occupied with cleaning up the broken glass in his bedroom, Tommy quietly opened the door leading from the kitchen to the rear garden. Closing the door as softly as he could, the boy walked to the spot where he had seen, or imagined he had seen, the five airmen first appear.

Within minutes he found what he was looking for, the object the bandaged man had dropped. He bent over, took a closer look, and recoiled. It was a human ear; a blood covered human ear. Recovering his composure, Tommy took out his handkerchief and used it to pick up the ear. Wrapping the ear in the handkerchief, he raced back to the house.

That afternoon, just as his mother had promised, several lorries pulled into the back garden of the house. By nightfall the wreckage had been cleared and even the broken fence repaired. From all outward appearances, nothing out of the ordinary had ever occurred.

3
FIFTY-FOUR YEARS LATER,
18 APRIL 1997: ARRIVAL AT GATWICK

Without warning the massive Boeing 747 shuddered, rose, fell, and then – just at the moment my stomach reached my throat – leveled off. The elderly blue-haired lady next to me woke with a start and grabbed my arm, her eyes wide with fear.

"Everything's okay," I assured her, praying that I was right, "we just ran into some turbulence. Nothing to worry about." She gave me a weak smile and, visibly embarrassed, released her death grip on my arm.

"Sorry about that folks," came a reassuring voice over the intercom, "just keep those ol' seat belts fastened. It won't be long now. Gatwick has cleared us for landing and we're on our final approach. Conditions at the airport are seven degrees Celsius, overcast, with light rain. And don't forget to turn your watches ahead. Today's the 18th in England and the local time is 7:35 a.m."

I opened the window shade and peered out. The sun was up, but I could make out nothing beneath the plane but clouds. I'd have to take the pilot's word that merry old England was down there ... somewhere. If memory served me, the last time I flew into London's Gatwick airport the visibility was just as bad. That was in the spring of 1972, with Jenny seated next to me. I had thought then that would be the last time I would be forced to visit this dreary, mildewed little country. I was wrong.

It was only because of Jenny's pleas that I had agreed to that trip a quarter century ago. Ironically, it's only because of her final request that I made this one. All that I could think was that the sooner I land and get this ordeal over with, the better.

One of the few things that Jenny and I ever seriously disagreed on was England. She, for reasons beyond me, loved the country and its people. Until the onset of her illness some five years ago, she would, like clockwork, return to the land of her birth for a six-week visit each summer. I, on the other hand, found the country to be, at best, disagreeable. But, most of all, I found the people insufferable. And, most unbearable of all was Bertie, Jenny's eccentric cousin.

Bertie will supposedly be at Gatwick to greet me. At least that's what he promised me in his email. If he keeps his word this would make it the first time in roughly thirty years that the loathsome little man has ventured outside London.

Jenny positively adored Bertie, although I could never understand why. Master of the inane, non-stop disseminator of trivia, tiresome ol' Cousin Bertie was the most awful bore I had ever encountered. Given the choice between a conversation with Bertie or blowing my brains out, I'd quickly find a proper, large-caliber weapon. Given the present circumstances, however, I would have no choice but to tolerate Cousin Bertie, at least until Jenny's request was honored.

For the past thirty or so years Bertie shared a tiny two bedroom flat with his mother on London's dingy Southside. His mother, Jenny's ill-tempered aunt Fiona, was an invalid and Bertie waited on her hand and foot. At least he did until her demise from cirrhosis of the liver about nine months ago – not a surprising fate considering Aunt Fiona's thirty yearlong love affair with cheap gin.

According to Jenny, Cousin Bertie once held some lofty goals and was considered by the family to be destined for great things. But that had all changed in the split second that the car that he, his father and his mother were in was run off the road by a drunken lorry driver – somewhere on the motorway between London and Oxford.

Bertie's father died on the spot. His mother suffered a fractured hip, an injury from which she never recovered. But Bertie, who had been driving, walked away without a scratch. In retrospect he – and the world – might have been better off had he shared his father's fate.

Bertie's injuries may not have been physical, but they were there … and they were evidently permanent. He never again drove a car. He dropped out of Oxford and devoted his life to taking care of Aunt Fiona and managing the musty little news agency under their flat. Other than that his only interests seemed to be drinking warm beer, watching birds (of, sadly, the non-human variety), and studying history, particularly military history.

If you can't find Bertie in his flat, or in the neighborhood pub, or at his news agency, you need look no farther than the park across the street. Bertie spends hours at a time there watching his feathered friends – most likely his only friends. His fascination with birds is passionate to the extreme, as would anyone who attempts to feed them soon find out. Cast even a single crumb in the direction of a hungry sparrow and Bertie – shaking and red faced with anger – will rise from his bench, point a menacing finger at you and demand you leave the park. Feeding wild animals, according to Bertie, is an unspeakable evil. That sort of behavior had, not surprisingly, ultimately earned Bertie the nickname of "Birdie" amongst his neighbors.

But maybe I'm being too hard on Bertie. After all, he had agreed – almost begged – to help me find Jenny's final resting place. One thing is sure; the odd little man loved Jenny.

#####

My not so fond reminisces of Cousin Bertie were interrupted by the squeal of the landing gear striking the runway, accompanied by the braking of the engines. Once the plane arrived at the gate and the all-clear signal chimed, I hurried to retrieve my one piece of carry-on luggage from the overhead bin. The thought of anyone else touching it sickened me.

Before departing Cleveland's Hopkins airport, yesterday, I had carefully wrapped the urn containing Jenny's ashes in bubble wrap, and then placed that precious container into a stiff cardboard box. To the box I duct-taped a makeshift rope handle. Opening the luggage compartment I retrieved the carton, relieved to see that everything was intact.

After reclaiming my checked luggage, Jenny's well-travelled roll-a-board, and clearing customs, I walked through the double doors into the dim and grimy Gatwick arrivals hall. I stood there for what seemed like several minutes before finally spotting Cousin Bertie, standing at the very rear of the crowd and looking uncharacteristically somber. When our eyes met he offered me an almost indiscernible wave. To my surprise, other than for a few gray hairs, Bertie looked much the same as he had nearly twenty-five years ago. I was almost certain he was wearing the same flat tweed cap and threadbare Harris Tweed jacket he wore then.

"Lo, Vince," said Bertie, offering me his hand and giving me the customary Englishman's dead fish handshake. "How was the flight?"

"It was all right, Bertie, and how are you doing? You're certainly looking well."

"I'm doing just fine," he responded, looking questioningly at the cardboard box. "Would that be Jenny? May I give you a hand?"

My first impulse was to say no, but the forlorn look on the man's face made me change my mind. I handed the box to Bertie. For just an instant he looked as if he was going to cry, then shook his head and stiffened his upper lip. Wouldn't do, I supposed, for a proper Englishman to show emotion, and it certainly appeared that Bertie was on the verge of losing control.

"So, Bertie, how do we get to your flat? Bus? Taxi?"

"Oh no, it's much cheaper and faster to take the train to Victoria Station. In fact I've already bought your ticket, as well as my return ticket. From there we hop on the tube."

"Fine," I answered. "Lead the way."

I followed Bertie down the escalators leading to the nondescript train station beneath the airport. Waiting there was the Gatwick Express – direct service to Victoria Station. I headed toward it, thinking that it must be the train Bertie had been talking about.

"No, Vince," said Bertie, "that's the express train. We'll be taking the regular commuter train. It may not be quite as fast, but it's a lot cheaper."

Cheap, I thought, just might be Bertie's middle name. According to Jenny, and even though she thought the world of Bertie, there were rumors that he still had the first shilling he had earned.

Our train arrived at the station a few minutes later. I'd have to say that it certainly looked a lot cheaper than the express. The train, in fact, looked like it was on its last legs. My guess was that the last time it had been maintained must have been during the Boer War. Worst of all it was covered in graffiti and dirt.

We clambered onto the train and were able to find a compartment with two empty, worn, and chewing gum encrusted seats. I managed to place the roll-a-board in an overhead rack and took my seat, facing Bertie. He, in turn, sat there holding onto the box containing Jenny's urn as if it were a newborn baby. The train ultimately pulled away from the station, and we inched ever so slowly toward Victoria Station.

Bertie was uncharacteristically quiet on the trip from Gatwick to his flat – at least other than for a half hour-long discourse on the history of Victoria Station. But even that was delivered in a subdued manner.

Even if I had wanted to listen to Bertie's monologue, it would have been difficult to impossible. It seemed as if everyone on the train had cell phones – or "mobiles" as the English insist on calling them, and each had either received or placed a call at the same time. With a train car full of people yelling into their cell phones, the noise level was incredible. Twenty-five years ago you could have heard a pin drop when riding the train or tube. On this day you would have trouble hearing yourself think. All I could think was that stuffy old England had definitely changed, for the worse – if that was possible.

The tube ride proved to be a repeat of the one experienced on the train, if not worse. Emerging from a putrid and decrepit underground station, and leaving the awful cell phone chatter behind, we walked the block or so to Bertie's flat – Bertie still carrying Jenny's urn, me dragging the roll-a-board.

A light rain was falling but that hadn't cleared the sidewalks of people. Every few yards there seemed to be clusters of humanity, huddled in groups in doorways and engaged in animated conversations. A few of them stopped talking when they saw Bertie, giving him the faintest hint of a greeting – and me an icy stare.

But these were definitely a different type of people than those who had been here in 1972. The proper Englishman in his jacket, wrinkled white shirt, and narrow dark tie seemed to have vanished, to be replaced by an astonishing number of Middle Easterners – virtually all of whom were men. Bertie and I appeared to be the only white faces on the street.

The neighborhood, which had been a bit shop-worn my last trip, now looked like some third world nation. Like the train stations we had passed on our journey from Gatwick, there was dirt, garbage and graffiti everywhere. A staggering number of crude, handwritten posters were affixed to walls, mailboxes, and lampposts. Again, however, Bertie seemed oblivious to the chaos about us.

Bertie's flat had, with one significant exception, hardly changed since my last visit. It was just as gloomy, chilly, and cramped as I remembered. I couldn't even begin to imagine what it must have been like to spend thirty long years there.

The one alteration to the living quarters was a flock of

cheaply constructed bookcases and file cabinets. They were on every wall of the living room, making the already diminutive flat seem even smaller. Either Bertie or his mother had been doing a lot of heavy reading over the past few decades. My bet was on Bertie.

Bertie pointed out what would be my bedroom for the night, his mother's former room, and suggested I deposit my luggage there. I opened the bedroom door and parked the roll-a-board in a corner.

The bedroom contained a narrow bed, nightstand, wardrobe and dressing table – but no bookcases or file cabinets, only a mountain of magazines stacked carefully on the floor next to the bed. All were, evidently, magazines about English royalty. Based on the stale smell that had engulfed me when I had entered, I suspected that the door to the room hadn't been opened in months. My spirits sank with the thought of spending the night there.

Returning to the living room, I watched as Bertie, his back to me, tenderly placed Jenny's cardboard box on a small coffee table in the living room. He then took a seat on the chair next to it, removed his glasses and brushed away what I suspected was a tear from his eye. It was only then that he realized I had returned. He quickly regained his composure.

"We'll leave tomorrow morning, Vince. You'll need a good night's rest after that long plane ride. But you best stay up till regular bedtime here, as I understand that's the proper way to deal with jet lag. Besides, we've got a lot of catching up to do. Have a seat and let's chat."

My mind reeled at that thought, but I nodded my head and took a seat on the couch. "You said you would make arrangements for a car. Where and when do we pick it up?"

"It's been taken care of," said Bertie, a strange faraway look in his eyes. "It's been taken care of; so don't you worry." With that he stood up and walked, grim-faced, to the window, the only window of the flat that faced the street. He stared into the distance for perhaps two minutes, then, shaking his head, turned to me. I feared a long discourse coming. I wasn't wrong.

"See those people out there?" asked Bertie, "Did you notice that not one of them is English?"

"Well," I answered, "they may not be the direct descendants of your Druids, Celts, Normans, or Anglo-Saxons, but I would guess they are English."

Bertie's eyebrows arched and he gave me a pitying look. "Perhaps on paper; perhaps on paper. But, sure as there's a God in Heaven, they aren't English in my eyes. Just look at them. They still dress like they did in the country they came from. Most still speak their native language – and damn few of them consider themselves English. Vince, you can walk for blocks and not see more than a handful of white faces.

I tried to restrain myself. I tried even harder not to let it show that the little bigot offended me. One thing I had learned in my previous encounters with Bertie was that there was little point in arguing with the man. It only prolonged his diatribes.

"Vince," Bertie continued, "did you notice the park across the street? There's graffiti, and worse, on every bench. Do you know what some of *those* people do? They actually trap and eat the birds, particularly the pigeons. Vince, those are not civilized human beings."

Clearly Bertie hadn't been as oblivious to the environment outside his flat as I had thought.

For the next hour or so Bertie lambasted his neighbors, moaned on about the dismal future of his country, damned the influx of American fast food joints, fumed about the EU, carped about the switch to the metric system, lamented the loss of manners in his country, and claimed that "those foreigners," as he called them, would be the downfall of England. Through it all I managed to maintain my silence, a prisoner in the tiny apartment. The thought of having to share a car with Bertie the next few days became more and more alarming.

"Bertie, jet lag or not, I've really got to get some sleep." I stood up, about to retreat to the sanctuary of the bedroom.

"I understand, Vince. But, before you do that we really do need to talk about the trip. Did you bring the painting?"

"No, Bertie, I didn't bring the painting, but I did have a full-sized color print made of it. I thought that a print would be easier to cart around the country. It's in my suitcase. Let me get it."

I placed the print on the kitchen table. Jenny's mother had painted the original when Jenny was about eight. It was quite beautiful, capturing an almost fairy tale landscape scene. In its center was a small church bathed in golden sunlight. To the left of the church, perhaps a hundred feet or so, was a cobalt blue brook. Two children were pictured on the bank of the stream. One, a chubby red-haired boy, was fishing. The other, a fair and delicate looking little girl, was picking wildflowers. The boy was supposedly Bertie, the girl, Jenny.

"Ah yes, that's the one. That's the church. It's been a long time but I do remember this painting. So it's there that our dear Jenny wants to rest?" Bertie said, pointing to the graveyard to the rear of the little church.

"Yes, just moments before she passed away she

pointed to the painting. Her last words to me were that I bury her there. I only wish she would have been able to tell me just where in the whole of England that little church might be located."

"Don't you worry, Vince, we'll find it. But I've got to ask you something. Jenny died nearly two years ago. Why is it that it's only now that you've brought her back for a proper burial?"

"You know, Bertie, you talk way too much. Way too damn much." A look of surprise and hurt came over Bertie's face. I strode to the bedroom and closed the door, immediately regretting my outburst.

4
SATURDAY MORNING, 19 APRIL 1997:
LONDON; THE QUEST BEGINS

The mounting din from the constant stream of cars, lorries, buses and ever so chatty people beneath the bedroom window woke me from a sound sleep. Not even the extra dose of painkillers I had taken the night before could have blocked out the clamor. No wonder Aunt Fiona had such a sour disposition. If I had to wake up every morning to this noise I'd start yelling at people too.

I looked at my watch. It was a few minutes before 6 a.m., London time, and – judging from the dim light coming through the curtained window – it appeared as though the sun had just begun to rise. Eager to get a start on the day, I turned on the lamp beside the bed. Its twenty-watt bulb lent the tiny room an unearthly hue. If Aunt Fiona used that pathetic little lamp to read all those magazines on the floor, she must have had one hell of a pair of eyes.

I put on my bathrobe, grabbed my ditty bag, and

opened the door. Bertie's bedroom door was ajar and the light coming from it illuminated the living room of his flat. I glanced into his bedroom and saw that it, like the living room, was absolutely chock-a-block with file cabinets and bookcases. Crammed into one corner was a small desk. Seated on that desk was a computer – a top of the line Dell with a twenty-inch screen. Bertie, it would seem, had embraced the Information Age – with a vengeance. The only things missing from his jam-packed bedroom was a bed – and Bertie.

"Morning, Vince," came a gravelly morning voice behind me.

I turned to see Bertie, reclining on the couch and propped on one elbow, rubbing the sleep from his eyes. "Bertie, I didn't realize you would have to sleep on the couch. You should have told me; I would have found a room for the night. I'm really sorry; I didn't know you had made your bedroom into an office."

"Think nothing of it, old chap. I've been sleeping on this sofa for about six years – ever since I ran out of space in the bedroom. It's really quite comfortable." He reached for a robe and pointed to the door of the flat's bathroom. "Go ahead and take care of things, Vince. I'll start breakfast." Looking at the clock, he added, "My goodness, we're going to get an early start on the day. That's good; lots to do. Lots to do."

Bertie's bathroom was so tiny that it reminded me of all the tired old jokes ever made about small rooms. But it was spotless and had all the necessary prerequisites. Stepping out of the shower I detected the unmistakable aroma of a full English breakfast, and my heart sank. After my unfortunate outburst last night, however, I didn't have it in me to tell Bertie that I despised fried tomatoes, loathed watery scrambled eggs, and could not stomach what passed for bacon in this sad country.

Bertie had set the table and poured tiny glasses of orange juice for the both of us. A big smile on his face, he remarked, "Have a seat, Vince; everything's ready." So I did, hoping that a full English breakfast may not have been quite as bad as I remembered. Unfortunately, it was worse.

In addition to the tomatoes, eggs, and bacon, Bertie had prepared tea, mushrooms, beans, fried bread, and black slabs of something I didn't recognize. Other than the hot tea and black slabs, which were only barely edible, everything else – including the "orange juice" – was just ghastly. Trying to be polite, I decided to ask him about the black slabs.

"Excellent breakfast, Bertie." His face lit up. "This meat or sausage, or whatever, was particularly tasty," I remarked, pointing at the last scrap of the black slabs.

"Ah," said Bertie, "so you like my black pudding. That's wonderful; most Yanks tend to shy away from it."

"Why's that?" I asked, hoping I could stomach the answer.

"I don't really know, Vince. I suppose it's just that the idea of eating congealed pig's blood wrapped in a length of pig's intestine puts some people off. You'd really think that a country that believes hotdogs are edible wouldn't be so squeamish." Pleased to no end by that witty observation, Bertie gave me a wink and shoveled in another spoonful of watery eggs.

I started to say something, thought better of it, and just nodded my head. Not much point in yelling at the man. Based on the amount of blood pudding he had ingested it was clear that Cousin Bertie considered the black garbage a delicacy.

When we were first married, Jenny had tried to tempt

me with a full English breakfast. That had resulted in our first spat. She was never able to convince me that English food was anything but sad garbage, although I have to admit that she did manage to train me to use certain English expressions. To this day the hood of a car is a "bonnet;" the trunk is a "boot;" and we always stopped at "petrol" stations, rather than gas stations, to have the car fueled or serviced. I never could, however, bring myself to call a wrench a "spanner" or a cookie a "biscuit."

It took Bertie at least two hours to wash, shave, dress and finish packing. I had the uneasy feeling that he wasn't really in a hurry to get this particular show on the road. It was ultimately agreed that we were going to be taking the print of the church, Jenny's urn, two suitcases, and three cardboard book boxes on our expedition.

"Bertie, what's with the boxes? Are we going to have room enough for all this?"

"I've got notes and reference materials in the boxes, Vince, and lots of ordnance survey maps. We'll need them if we're going to find that church. Mark my words."

I shrugged my shoulders, deciding not to argue with him. "So, where do we pick up the car?"

"Abdul should be around any minute now," said Bertie, looking at the clock over the kitchen stove. It was almost 10 a.m. I didn't ask who Abdul was.

At precisely 10 a.m. there was a single, sharp knock on the rear door of the flat. Bertie opened the door and I could see two men, one evidently an Arab, the other a tall, muscular black man. Both seemed delighted to see Bertie. Both eyed me with suspicion.

The Arab was indeed Abdul. The black man was named Nigel. Judging from his accent, I guessed he was from some Caribbean island, probably Jamaica.

Between the four of us we gathered up the suitcases

and boxes. Nigel, effortlessly carrying two of the book boxes, headed out the back door, down the rickety steps, and into the rear garden. The rest of us followed his lead.

There was a small alley directly behind the garden, a place where I would have expected the rental car to be parked. There wasn't, however, an automobile in sight. Instead of heading toward the alley, Nigel strode purposely toward an ancient, dilapidated garden shed and placed his boxes on the ground. Abdul put his box down and tossed Nigel a huge brass key, roughly the size of a man's fist. Nigel then quickly opened the oversize lock on the door of the shed, grinning like a madman, his teeth flashing in the morning light.

There wasn't a single garden tool in the shed, but there was what appeared to be an undersized car – covered for the moment in old bed sheets. Nigel walked to one side of the car, Abdul to the other. They looked to Bertie, who simply nodded his head. On the count of three the two men removed the covering with a flourish. All that was missing was a drum roll.

What I saw when the sheets were removed literally took my breath away. It was a small, incredibly shiny black car – appearing to be a relic from either the thirties or, at best, post Second World War. I was speechless.

Abdul broke the silence. "So, Professor, how do you like it? Quite a beauty, don't you think?"

"It is definitely beautiful," I responded, and I meant it. "But do you think a car of this age is going to be reliable … and safe?" The smiles disappeared from the faces of Abdul and Nigel. I had clearly committed a major *faux pas*.

I turned to Bertie, who just rolled his eyes. "Vince, this is quite possibly the finest motorcar ever manufactured. This, my dear man, is a 1949 two-door Morris Minor MM

Saloon. Abdul and Nigel have spent months of nights and weekends working on the car. It's been licensed, registered, and road tested. It may be a little long in the tooth, but it will take us anywhere we want to go, and quite reliably and safely I'm sure."

Nigel chimed in. "Only eight thousand miles on the car, mon, and those are brand new tires. Michelins. Brand new hoses and fan belts too." Abdul nodded in agreement.

Bertie, his face now red with either anger or embarrassment, walked to the front of the car and opened the bonnet. Inside was the smallest engine I had ever seen in an automobile.

"This," Bertie said, pointing to the pint-sized engine, "is a 918cc sidevalve engine – arguably the most reliable engine ever produced. This car has an Alta DIY conversion kit giving it a top speed of 78 mph and a 0-60 time of 20.4 seconds. All that and 40 mpg on the highway." With that he slammed the bonnet shut.

A top speed of 78 mph? A 0-60 time of 20.4 seconds? My God, I thought, we'd have trouble racing a snail. Yet Bertie and his two lunatic chums seemed to think this relic of the forties was safe to drive on the motorways of the nineties.

THE LAST ENGLISH VILLAGE IS AVAILABLE IN BOTH PAPERBACK AND EBOOK FORMAT.

GO TO
http://bentspurtx.wix.com/jamesignizio
FOR FURTHER INFORMATION.

Made in the USA
Lexington, KY
23 December 2017